HORIZON
PREDATORS OF EDEN
ALPHA

D1360589

D.W. VOGEL

Horizon Alpha: Predators of Eden

Future House Publishing

ISBN-10: 1-944452-25-7
ISBN-13: 978-1-944452-25-4

Developmental editing by Emma Hoggan
Substantive editing by Mandi Diaz
Copy editing by Jenna Parmley
Interior design by Samuel Millar

To Chef Vogel

BEFORE EDEN

We never would have come to this planet if we'd known.

If Earth's scientists had had more time to study the skies, they might have realized. But there wasn't any time. Their first report of Mercury's wobble projected that Jupiter's gravity would pull Earth's neighbor out of orbit in only eighty years. Eighty years until Earth would be destroyed. They had less than a century to build the Horizon fleet, four city-sized Arks. Less than a century to choose four potentially habitable worlds and equip the Arks to be self-sufficient for generations. To figure out how to propel a ship the size of a small town across the galaxy to a brand new planet. To choose the lucky group of refugees who would carry the seeds of our doomed species.

That was two hundred years ago.

All four Horizon ships left Earth's orbit, and because Tau Ceti e was the closest habitable planet, our distant ancestors on the Alpha ship had the shortest journey. Even then, when they boarded Horizon Alpha for the one-way voyage, they knew they would never set foot on solid ground again. Generations were born, lived, and died aboard the city-size ship, breathing the recycled air of a dead planet. They kept busy: they read and played games, they grew crops in the gardens, and they bred sheep, the only farm animal deemed useful enough to devote space to. They trained the next generation of scientists to spend years studying how two centuries in space would affect all the living things they brought from Earth. They fought the despair that must have plagued all those unfortunates who knew they wouldn't live to see the new world, humanity's last hope.

Our ancestors were still luckier than most. Horizon Gamma never made it out of Earth's solar system. Every year we take a moment of silence on Day 45 for Gamma's five hundred souls and Day 138 for the billions more who never got to leave Earth at all. The Beta and Delta are still out there somewhere, speeding toward distant stars and other worlds.

At least, we think they are.

It's been over a century since the distance between our ships ended communications, but neither of them was scheduled for planetfall for at least another 300 Earth years.

Ceti's orbit is faster than Earth's, so we get just under three hundred days a year here. We're a bit closer to our sun than Earth was, and a lot bigger. It's hotter here day and night, and Ceti is younger than Earth. In the panic to get humans off our home world, nobody realized what those conditions might mean when they pointed us here.

By the time Horizon entered orbit around Tau Ceti e, it was far too late to turn back. We had only enough fuel to get here and set up a preliminary city. The long-dead scientists of Earth expected us to figure out the natural resources here and sort out a new life for ourselves. They must have envisioned a preindustrial society, Earth's descendants making campfires and living off a new land.

We never blamed them. They meant well.

After centuries of travel, Horizon Alpha arrived. We launched probes to test the atmosphere and found it oxygen-rich and clean. Our sensors sent back data that told us of a warm, damp planet teeming with plant and animal life. We had no way to know what the plants would be like, but we had crops and seeds on Horizon to sow this new world with familiar foods. We had dreams of domesticating the animals, whatever they might turn out to be. Surely this was a new Eden, a garden of plenty where humanity would thrive.

I was born twelve years before we entered Ceti's orbit. My brother, Josh, was four years old then, and my mom had just completed her medical training. And our dad was captain of the Horizon Alpha. We were the lucky ones. The first humans in generations to set foot on the natural soil of a living planet.

Horizon herself was far too large to make planetfall, but we had plenty of shuttles to carry us and everything we'd need down to our new home. My father would be the last man to leave the ship. He would engage the solar-powered autopilot that would keep Horizon in geosynchronous orbit, our eternal eyes-in-the-sky above our proposed base.

The plan was to deploy our communication satellites and scan the planet to determine the best place to land, but the satellites showed us images of dense jungles, wide rivers, and vast oceans. We couldn't see past the thick canopy and had no idea what animals had evolved here, but we were thrilled to finally be so close to the end of our journey.

We started loading a single shuttle to send to the planet's surface. The team inside would scout out the planet while we waited for their report.

Moments before the shuttle took off, an explosion rocked Horizon's hull.

The shock wave pulsed right through my shoes. Sirens blared and lights flashed.

"Emergency evacuation. All personnel report to your transport shuttle for immediate departure." The robotic voice repeated the message over and over.

Mom told Josh and me to grab everything we could carry from our home unit and run for the shuttle. We were assigned to transport 36, halfway across the width of Horizon. People were running everywhere, babies screamed, and the air started to smell thick. Josh carried my little sister, Malia, and we pushed through the crowds toward our evacuation assignment.

"Where's Dad?" I yelled in the chaos, even though I knew he was probably in the control room, keeping the ship flying.

When we got to bay 36, the shuttle was gone. One of Horizon's officers herded us onto the next shuttle, and we crammed in as tightly as we would fit. We all got seats and belted ourselves in, but more people kept boarding and there wasn't enough room. My ears popped when they closed the shuttle doors and the cabin changed pressure.

And then we were falling.

I looked out the window to see Horizon in the black sky above us, before the window was obscured by fire as we entered Ceti's atmosphere. I thought the burn would last forever as the little ship bucked and shook. Finally the window cleared, the engines kicked on, and we were flying high above a green world.

Ceti is larger than Earth, so its gravity is stronger. We were supposed to fly in formation to an orderly landing, all the shuttles together. But we were losing altitude too fast. The pilot kept us in the air as long as he could, searching for an open field to land in. Finally he saw a likely spot, and we raced for the ground.

The final leg of our one-way trip was over, and as we bumped to a halt on the ground, Mom started to cry.

"It's okay, Mom, we landed. We're all right."

She shook her head and clutched Malia so hard that she started to cry, too, huge tears on her little cheeks. I tried to comfort her, but I didn't understand why she was crying.

Somehow Mom knew when we landed that Dad wouldn't leave his damaged ship. Our shuttle's pilot told Mom that Dad had sent out a final message of hope to all the shuttles that had escaped Horizon, and that he loved us very much. In the three years since, Mom has never mentioned his name again.

Seven of the launched ships landed in the riverside clearing that became Eden base. Three of them were huge transports like the one we were on, and four more were small shuttles intended to go back and forth to Horizon as we removed all its contents and set up our new home.

We had brief satellite contact with a few of the other transports, but they were scattered across the planet, too far to join us here. I don't know if any of them survived. There might be other settlements elsewhere on Ceti, but if they're out there, we haven't heard from them.

In those first moments, though, I was mostly just relieved. I craned my neck to see out the window.

It was all right. We had landed safely.

We were here.

I tried to stand up and fell back into my seat. Gravity was pulling on me just like it did the shuttles. I was heavier than I had ever been on the artificial gravity of Horizon. I hauled myself up, gripping the seat in front of me with leaden arms.

The huge bay doors opened and I smelled fresh air for the first time in my life. It smelled green and wet and alive, and I wanted to run out and bury my hands in the dirt, to immerse myself in this solid new world.

A roar echoed through the shuttle. Our pilot slammed the bay doors closed and everyone pressed toward the nearest window, straining to see through the thick glass.

We felt the vibration of the footfalls and everyone went silent. I can still hear the voice of the first person who saw it and realized what it was.

"Sweet shining stars, it's a dinosaur!"

CHAPTER 1

Sweat beaded on my forehead and trickled down the back of my neck as I lined up with the rest of my unit. The youngest member of Eden's pathetic army, I stood rigid under the blazing sun, trying to look more mature than my fifteen years. A giant bloodsucker mosquito buzzed past my ear and settled on my upper lip. I snorted, trying to blow it away with quick puffs of breath, not daring to break formation to swat it.

"Count off," General Carthage ordered.

Down the line of boys, we called out our names.

"Caleb Wilde, ready!" I barked when it was my turn.

Behind me, the shuttle's door gaped open and heat poured off the grungy metal wings.

A distant roar echoed down the valley and every head jerked toward the sound. Across the river, a gargling shriek cut off mid-squeal.

Inside the shuttle, Pilot Bronton ignited the thrusters, drowning out the General's next words. The vibration rumbled across our small electrified haven within the towering jungle. The General waved us toward the shuttle's rusty hatch and we trooped forward. I flicked the engorged bloodsucker off my lip with a wet snap of my finger.

I stumbled as a small pair of arms wrapped around my leg from behind.

"Malia, come here this instant!" Mom's voice carried over the whine of the thrusters.

I crouched low and my little sister threw herself around my neck. Her tears mingled with the sweat on my cheek. I picked her up, hugging her tight. The sun had bleached her pale hair to almost white and had darkened my skin to the brown color of tree bark. Together we made light and shadow; Malia was the starlight in my night sky.

"It's okay, Mali. I'll be home in time for dinner," I said.

Her blue eyes searched mine faithlessly and my smile faded. Our brother, Josh, had told her that, too, when he left on a mission three months ago.

"I promise." I started to peel her sticky limbs off my skin. "Mali, what do we say? 'However long the stars shine . . .'" I began the words our dad had always said, our family's motto.

She sniffled. ". . . that's how long I love you."

Mom rushed up to take her, and Malia clung to her, sobbing. Mom's dry eyes and dark face betrayed no emotion. Her gaze flickered past my shoulder, and a presence loomed behind me.

"I'll take care of him, Randa," the General said.

My mom nodded and my face burned. I was a full soldier now. Nobody needed to take care of me.

My mother had been livid when the General told her he was taking me on this mission to retrieve the reactor core.

"Absolutely not. I've already lost a husband and one son.

You are not taking Caleb!" I'm sure the whole base heard her screaming at him. The General and my mom had argued for days about it, and the General won. I couldn't hear what he said to her, and I don't know how he convinced her, but he must have promised I'd be safe with him. It rankled me a little bit because this was probably the safest and easiest mission I could go on, and everyone was still treating me like a child. But I was happy for the General's insistence because I was flying out on the shuttle. No amount of crying from my mom or baby sister would sway him.

"I'll be okay, Mom," I added. "It's just a few hours' flight. Nothing can get us in the sky."

Her lips pressed into a thin line and she nodded. She had already hugged me goodbye this morning, clutching me as if she were drowning.

Now she clenched her jaw as she turned away from the idling shuttle. Malia didn't look up from weeping, her face buried in mom's hair.

The General's hand clapped my shoulder and I started, tearing my eyes away from the only family I had left.

"It's time to go, son," he said.

I'm not your son.

I hated it when he talked like that. I looked up to the General, respected him, and was as intimidated by him as anyone else in Eden was. But my mom had never been afraid of him, and after Josh disappeared, he'd moved in with us. He said he wanted to take care of my mom until I was old enough to be the man of the house. I knew Mom wanted me to accept him as part of the family, and my little sister Malia had slipped and called him "daddy" a few times, but I had pretended not to hear.

Back on Horizon or long ago on Earth, a fifteen-year-old would still be considered a child, but here in Eden we grew up fast. I hoped this mission would convince Mom that I was old enough for us not to need another dad around, and maybe she'd make him move out. It was selfish of me but I didn't care. No one could ever replace my dad or brother. I didn't want the General to try.

The idling thrusters roared to life as I stepped onto the shuttle's retracting metal stairs. The hinges creaked under my boots, and I pulled myself through the hatchway.

I peeked over my shoulder as the General swung the heavy door shut behind me, but Mom was already out of sight. I thought she'd stay and wave at us as we lifted off, but I guess she couldn't stand to watch.

Never mind. Nothing was going to spoil the day I had dreamed about for three long years. Today I became a real soldier. I lifted my chin and grinned as my eyes adjusted to the shuttle's dim interior.

"You're next to me, rookie," said Jack. At eighteen, he was a veteran of several missions outside the fences, and had been one of my brother's closest friends. He patted the seat next to him, and I smiled a little wider. He'd let me have the window.

I stumbled over his legs as the shuttle lurched off the ground. My butt smacked into the seat, and I scrambled to snap the pitted buckle of my harness. A faint smell of mold hit my nostrils as I pulled on the straps.

The thrusters roared, making further conversation impossible as our little shuttle strained to overcome gravity. Outside the thick glass window, the high wire fences of Eden base fell away as we sputtered into the blue sky. The little clearing disappeared behind us, with the rusting hulks of our huge transports arranged in a wide circle with electrified wire strung between them. Our safe haven on the bank of the swollen brown river looked so small from above.

The trees that looked so huge from below made an unbroken carpet of green beneath us as we flew. Our shuttle couldn't get much higher than the top of the lush canopy, but we picked up speed and soared over the rolling hills.

The engines quieted as we reached our cruising altitude.

Jack punched me in the shoulder. "First time off base!"

"Yeah," I said, "but I don't think we'll get to see much. We're only going to be out a few hours."

"Let's hope so," Jack said.

After three long years confined inside the cramped perimeter of the fences, my nerves jumped like a prisoner just released from jail. I took deep breaths of the mildew-scented air. It reminded me of the first twelve years of my life, breathing Horizon's recycled atmosphere as we hurtled through space toward this dense green planet.

Trees whizzed by underneath us, and I peered across the landscape, hoping for a glimpse of animal life from a safe distance. The shuttle cast a triangular shadow on the canopy below us, but only wind stirred the leaves.

The soldiers across the aisle pointed at something outside their window. I ripped off my seat harness and jumped up to see what they were looking at.

"What's down there?" I called to them, but they didn't hear me over the shuttle's rumbling.

"What's down there?" Jack echoed, quirking an eyebrow at me.

I flopped back into my seat and pressed my face against the window.

"Calm down, rookie," Shiro said from the seat behind me. "It's a two hour flight and you're making me crazy. Just be glad we're flying and not walking."

I laughed. Our destination was much too far away for a land-based mission. Walking would be suicide. Still, I was embarrassed that Shiro had to settle me down.

"I'm just glad I'm not stuck in a classroom anymore. Even if we don't see anything out here, it's better than lessons," I said.

"True." Jack reached over to pull the seat harness back over my head.

"I got it," I mumbled, strapping myself back in.

The General strode down the aisle between the seats. We all sat up straighter as he passed. His footing was secure on the bumpy shuttle, eyes appraising his young soldiers.

"Does he know where we're going?" I whispered.

"They have the coordinates," Jack said. "I just hope we can find the core when we get there."

"We'll find it," I said. "I promised Malia I'd be home for dinner."

Jack nodded but didn't answer. He didn't have to. We both knew that was a risky promise to make.

CHAPTER 2

"Look alive troops, we've got fliers!"

The General paced in the shuttle's open cockpit. I couldn't see his face from my seat in the hold but we all turned to look out the dirty windows toward the distant treetops below us. I unbuckled my seat harness again and leaned forward to get a better view.

The shuttle banked hard to starboard and I fell into Jack's lap.

"Sit down, rookie." He gave me a friendly shove. "Buckle back up before you hurt yourself."

But I didn't want to miss a thing.

The only time I had flown before was on the way down from the Horizon three years ago. I had never seen pterosaurs from above, only watched them circling high overhead, screeching their raspy calls into the steamy air.

"Sorry." I buckled my shoulder belt, stretching forward to look down as the shuttle took an abrupt dive. My breakfast jumped up into my throat for a sickening minute.

Pilot Bronton was talking to the General, who gripped the metal support post behind the pilot's chair.

"I've never seen them this agitated before, sir. They usually hear us coming and keep clear."

"Well, they're not keeping clear today." The General crouched down to look up through the windshield. "They're everywhere."

A dark shadow passed over the pilot's instruments seconds before a huge brown body soared right over the top of our shuttle. The wind from the enormous wings buffeted our little ship and we lurched in the sky. My knuckles turned white as I clutched my seat harness.

"Scat them! What are they doing?" The General had fallen across his jump seat and now grudgingly strapped himself in.

A female voice spoke up from the front row. "Sir, I think . . . I think it's a dominance flight."

"Dominance?" The General swung around in his seat to face the woman who had spoken, and I leaned forward to see our naturalist, Sara Arnson. She was one of my teachers at the Eden base school I graduated from last month. I wondered what on Ceti a naturalist was doing with a bunch of soldiers, but Shiro and Jack looked unconcerned. Don't ask another stupid question.

Instead, I looked as far behind us as my harness would allow and saw two more huge forms winging in from right below us. The triangular heads were focused on each other and they passed close enough for me to see the flat black eyes in their scaled faces. They paid us no attention, but the shuttle bounced again from their turbulent wingbeats.

"There must be a female nearby." Ms. Arnson craned her neck to see out the windows.

The female was flying over the distant treetops. The males around us were dwarfed by the solitary female soaring and diving in the humid updrafts. She was surrounded by a swarm of males, the entourage flying uncomfortably closer to our little craft. I watched the males dive-bombing each other, chasing the younger ones away from the female they all circled.

Ms. Arnson spoke again. "They think we're a rival male. I think they're trying to chase us away from the female. I've never seen the behavior before, but I've read about this kind of thing in Earth animals."

The General scowled and looked around with steely anger for someone to blame. "We'll give them a wide berth, then. They can fight or fly or do whatever they want without us. Come around from the port side instead of straight on," he ordered the pilot. I flinched under the General's glare and dropped my gaze into my lap. Jack ground his teeth in the seat next to me, staring straight ahead.

The shuttle banked hard again and the g-forces pinned me into my seat.

Bright afternoon sun blinded me as we swung around to avoid the fliers. We had plenty of daylight, which was good since the shuttle's lights had quit working last year. We had been late getting out this morning because of a code T threat on the west fence, but our target was only two hours away on a good wind. The shuttle was half-empty as we didn't intend to be on the ground long enough to need much firepower. The General and the pilot, the naturalist Sara Arnson, me, and eight other soldiers all bounced in our seats as another flier passed way too close.

"Why are they still following us?" the General demanded. "We turned away from her territory." The female was nearly out of sight, but three males still swooped around us, the wind from their wings knocking our shuttle around like toy boats on a wild river.

One of the males dove right into another, impacting hard with the huge muscles of his neck. The collision tore the smaller male's wing, and the beast plummeted toward the ground in a sickening spiral.

"They're not just chasing each other. They're fighting for dominance. They're knocking each other right out of the sky."

Ms. Arnson's voice was high and strained.

My pulse pounded loud in my throat. Ms. Arnson knew more about these creatures than anyone else in Eden. And she sounded scared.

The thrusters whined as the pilot raced ahead, trying to outfly the two remaining males. I clutched the seat in front of me as the shuttle careened through the sky. My stomach rolled, threatening to return my breakfast. I did not want to throw up in front of the rest of the team. I'd never hear the end of it if I vomited on my very first flight.

A sharp impact rattled the ship and the crunch of metal echoed in the confined space. One of the males had clipped us.

"General, we've lost the port thruster. I need to set down now!" Pilot Bronton angled the shuttle into a steep dive, and I felt light in my seat as we raced for the ground. The sputter of the damaged thruster warred with the noise of my heartbeat vibrating in my ears. My dry mouth tasted like bile.

"This is not a good location. We're too far from the target. Retreat to Eden base." The General sounded angry.

I kept looking out the window. Settle down, stomach. Don't throw up.

The pilot shouted above the screaming engine. "Negative, General. We'll never make it back with those fliers on our tail."

"Dammit, Bronton, if we set down here we'll never take off again!"

My head slammed into the window as the flier hit us from the side. I tasted blood and my vision blurred.

The General yelled for Bronton to pull up, the shuttle spinning down toward the forest canopy below us. Ms. Arnson's screams echoed through the hold as we crashed through the thick branches.

"Mayday, Mayday!" Bronton's voice yelled from the cockpit. "No satellite, they're not hearing us!"

The trees slowed our fall but not enough. The shuttle rolled as it slid across the forest floor. Metal shrieked as the shuttle's entire port side tore away and empty space replaced the seats where soldiers had been sitting. My hands clutched the straps of my harness and my head bounced off the shuttle window.

We're gonna die.

The crash seemed to go on for hours. When we finally spun to a halt, the open gash in the shuttle faced the sky through a hole in the thick canopy. In the moment before I blacked out, I saw the pterosaur males circle over our heads, then soar away into the cloudless blue sky.

CHAPTER 3

Dull throbbing pain woke me, pulsing through my chest and shoulders. I'm not dead. How am I not dead?

Jack had slumped over his seat onto me, his shoulder harness broken and dangling in front of my face. My shoulder ached from where he was crushing me into the window of the ruined shuttle. He wasn't moving.

"Jack," I pushed at him, trying to reach my harness buckle. My ears rang and I couldn't hear anyone else talking. "Jack," I said louder, and he stirred and moaned.

Thank goodness. He's not dead, either.

"Hurts," he rasped.

"I know, but you gotta get off me. We need to get out of

here."

Even through the haze of pain and dizziness, I knew we had to move. Every 'saur for kilometers must have heard the crash. With the side of the shuttle torn wide open over our heads, we were a popped can of lunch for the first to arrive. I had no idea how long I'd been unconscious, but it couldn't have been long because I didn't smell any 'saurs and didn't see any huge open mouths reaching in to pluck us out of our seats.

Jack groaned and rolled off me, and I managed to unbuckle my seat harness. I crouched on the window underneath me, looking up at the clear blue sky. At least four of my fellow soldiers had been in the seats that ripped away when we crashed. I'd been raised with those guys, known them since I was born. Please, let them have died on impact. The alternative was so much worse.

I did a quick mental check of my status. A knot on my forehead was already starting to swell up but wasn't bleeding. My shoulders ached from the seat harness. My legs felt wobbly from the aftermath of the adrenaline shock, but on the whole I was intact and functional.

I stood up to peek over the seats. The General was just getting to his feet. He leaned over to where the pilot slumped and touched the man's neck. His hand came away bloody and the General shook his head.

"What happened?" Ms. Arnson's weak voice was barely audible.

I ducked under Jack, who had started unstrapping himself, and crawled over the empty row of seats in front of me. Ms. Arnson was alive, and so were Shiro and Brent, the two other soldiers who had been sitting on my side of the shuttle. They were starting to stir in the seats behind me. The General climbed back from the cockpit to join us.

"Count off," he said quietly.

Shiro and Brent both said their names as they struggled to their feet in the overturned hold.

"Caleb Wilde, here," I said.

"Jack Branch, here," Jack said behind me.

"Sara Arnson, here." She hadn't even tried to stand, just hung there in her seat harness.

The General crouched down in front of her and started to unbuckle her. "You need to stand up, Sara. We need to grab what we can and get out of here. It's not safe in daylight."

We all knew it wasn't safe at night, either, but I didn't say it aloud.

We hadn't planned on an overnight mission. We didn't have much survival gear packed, but we gathered up the weapons and supplies strewn around the hold, strapping on our ammunition with shaking hands. I grabbed a canvas pack and hoisted it onto my back, and we all waited for the General's order. At his command, we crawled over the last of the seats and ducked into the cockpit.

The windshield of the shuttle had shattered on impact, and I peeked at the dead pilot as I crawled past him. A large shard of the glass had slashed his throat, and he hung limp in his seat. His dangling arm brushed against my back as I approached the broken windshield, and the touch chilled me.

"Fly free, Bronton," I whispered to his corpse as I wiggled out of the shuttle.

I followed Ms. Arnson and the rest of the team away from the wreckage and turned to see Jack struggling through the opening, the last to leave the crash. A long gash ripped through the front of his fatigue pants and blood soaked his leg.

"Come on, buddy," I encouraged him, dropping back to slip my arm under his shoulder. His leg wouldn't bear much weight, but I helped him hobble into the clearing where Shiro and Brent waited with Ms. Arnson and the General. They were all cut and battered, and Brent's left eye was starting to swell shut, but Jack had the most urgent injury.

He sat down heavily on the ground and the General opened his pack. Jack stifled a cry as clean bandages were wound tightly around his leg. I hoped it would slow the bleeding. I shuddered to think of how quickly a 'saur could track us if we left a blood trail.

The General stood and faced us. "We went down close to

our target. We'll get to the site as fast as we can and call for help from Eden base. They'll send another shuttle to pick us up from the target site. We didn't have sat coverage, so our mayday didn't go through, and the tree cover is too dense for them to land here anyway."

Shiro glanced over my shoulder at the ruined shuttle. "General, should we . . . should we go back and try to find the others?"

Four soldiers had been sitting on the left side of the shuttle, and were ripped away as we crashed to the forest floor. Viktor and Raj weren't much older than me. We also lost Cara's dad and Mr. Hague, who taught me how to shoot a rifle.

Nobody could have survived that impact.

The General echoed my thought. "We're not going back." He sighed. "If I thought we might find them alive . . . but no. We can't risk the mission searching for our dead. There will be time to grieve when we're safe behind the wire again."

Silently, we began the hike. We took turns supporting Jack limping through the forest. The General led the way, trying to check our location on his satellite transmitter, but the thick tree canopy blocked his signal. My pack rode hot on my back, and my fatigues were sticking to my skin. I hoped we weren't too far.

The sun was still much too high in the sky. It would be safer at night, but sunset was still a few hours away. The most dangerous of Ceti's dinosaurs were daytime hunters.

Okay, they aren't really dinosaurs.

True dinosaurs lived on Earth and have all been dead for sixty million years. The animals who evolved here in this steamy jungle share no blood with Earth's ancient rulers. Ms. Arnson had more scientific names for most of the species we'd encountered on Ceti, carefully drawn in her little sketchbook. But when you face a three-story reptilian predator with a head the size of your shuttle that walks on its hind legs and knocks down trees with the swipe of a forty-foot tail, there's just nothing you can call it besides T-rex.

Most of the 'saurs here went torpid at night, their smaller

bodies losing heat quickly after sunset. It never got really cold, but Ms. Arnson taught us in school that their metabolism depended on staying a lot warmer than our body temperature. Only the largest had enough mass to retain the necessary heat all night, besides a few of the little fliers that relied on friction to stay warm. The rest went to ground at dark to hide from the biggest predators. Some covered themselves with leaves and soil to evade the Rex's heat sensors, which detected a 'saur's cooling body temperature.

A few of the bigger herbivores were active at night, but as long as we stayed out from under their huge, crushing feet, they wouldn't be a danger to us. Daytime was another matter.

We were easy prey outside the fence. Gila venom could kill a man within ten steps. They weren't particularly fast, but they sat so still in the underbrush that you didn't realize you were too close until it was too late and their poison-loaded tails were swinging around to stab you. The huge, camouflaged Crabs were also a risk, but they were invisible day or night, so we wouldn't avoid them either way.

But the real danger was the Wolves. Named for Earth's pack-hunting mammals, our 'saur Wolves ran on four legs. They traveled in family groups, sniffing the air for prey and running it down from all sides. A small pack of them could take down the largest brachiosaur with a coordinated effort. If a Wolf pack found our trail, this mission was over.

Since I was born on a space ship, the first twelve years of my life were spent dreaming about solid ground, about the planet we were heading for. My first steps on solid ground weren't the triumphant strides I had imagined in my childhood. They were a frightened skitter between ships in the dark of night.

In the first weeks after we came down from Horizon, we lost over fifty men to 'saur attacks. Their deaths taught us about Gila poison and Wolf packs. We learned which snakes had the strongest venom, and that if a human ventured into the river, something huge would swallow him in one gulp.

We had tried to find somewhere safer to settle, but we lost so many scout teams that we had to stop sending them. General

Carthage assumed command of our base. He ended the search for survivors and concentrated on making Eden base more secure. We circled the ships and ran wire between them, and the dinosaurs learned they shouldn't mess with electricity.

All the men trained for the army. Women were deemed too valuable, since the future of our species depended on having enough babies to continue our population. With the frozen embryos that made it safely off Horizon, men weren't as important, so we were the ones who took the risks. We scouted from the air when we could, hunting for food and trying to learn more about the area. But our heavy shuttles flew low over the treetops, their range limited by Eden's more intense gravity.

My brother Josh went out on one of those missions. The soldiers took enough ammunition and supplies on their mission to be gone for a week. None of his team made it back.

My first mission as a soldier was heading to a crash site, a transport that hadn't survived the escape from Horizon Alpha. It carried a reactor fuel core, and Eden needed the power desperately.

Eden had solar cells, but we didn't have room for enough panels in our tiny wired enclosure to supply the electricity required to keep the base safe from the huge predators intent on eating us. Since we landed, our few engineers had also been trying to harness the power of a fast-flowing river at the base of the mountain range in Eden's backyard, but every time they thought the hydropower turbines were foolproof, something knocked them out.

The reactor core was the only thing powerful enough to keep the fences charged while we figured out some kind of long-lasting energy source, or found somewhere else to live on this planet, somewhere that wasn't overrun with dinosaurs. In theory, there were five more fuel cores scattered around the planet, but this was the only one we knew of in flying distance, and without it, Eden's power wouldn't last another month. Once we returned with the power core, we'd have a few months more to figure out a long term solution.

"How's Jack doing up there?" Shiro asked from behind me. He was bringing up the rear and kept whipping his head around to check the trail we were making.

"I'm fine," Jack answered through gritted teeth. "You don't have to talk about me like I'm not here. I'm not dead yet."

"Will you two shut up?" Brent mumbled from in front of us. He was creeping through the forest so close to the General's heels I thought he might crawl right into the General's faded uniform with him. The image of that, of Brent and the General buttoned together in one set of fatigues, made me smile. Jack clutched my shoulder and I focused on the path they blazed in front of me.

We jumped at every sound. The forest was loud with the screeching calls of the smaller reptiles that lived here. That was a good sign. If a larger predator were near, the little ones would fall silent. But every bush that rustled and every little creature that raced away from us made us tense up and raise our weapons. I peered into the dense underbrush, my palm slick against the butt of my pistol.

Nobody here, just ignore us, I silently willed to any 'saur that might be nearby. My hand was shaking so badly I doubted I would be able to pull the trigger if anything burst through the forest into our path. Big brave soldier Caleb.

The General kept trying his satellite transmitter as we made our way through the steamy forest. We paused at a swift, flowing stream to fill our canteens and wash some of our smaller abrasions. We kept Jack out of the water, not wanting to reopen his seeping leg wound.

It was weird to see him struggling. He'd always been first for everything. Three years ago when our long space journey was over and we finally saw solid ground for the first time, Jack couldn't wait to get off the shuttle that brought us down from the Ark. He'd pushed through the crowd of adults straining toward the first breath of non-recycled air any of us had ever smelled; the first generation in two hundred years to stand on an actual world.

Jack leaned on my shoulder now, heavier with each step we took.

As the light began to fail, we found the crash site we had come for. Three years in the foliage had nearly covered the remains of the huge transport, but we hacked at the vines with our knives until we found an entry door. The metal screamed a protest as we forced the door open on rusting hinges. The interior of the transport was pitch black, but we all piled in, closing the door behind us. I turned on my flashlight and aimed the beam around the space, making sure we were alone. No red eyes reflected back at me and we all relaxed.

We set up this mission with the hope that the original passengers, if they had survived the crash, hadn't taken the reactor core with them. If they had, it was lost forever. Which meant this mission, already a disaster with five dead soldiers and a crashed shuttle, would be a total failure.

CHAPTER 4

Even though the door on the transport had been rusted shut, the smell told us that something lived in here. The smell took a moment to identify, but when Brent identified the warm, musty scent as wet fur, we all relaxed. Shrews lived here, not dinosaurs. The mammalian inhabitants of this world weren't really shrews, but they were small and furry and darted around the jungle at night. And they wouldn't nest anywhere a dinosaur could get inside.

The air was thick with insects. I slapped ineffectively at the bloodsuckers who thought my neck was a feast.

Jack sat on a decaying crate near the closed door, and the rest of us spread out, searching in the dark for the fuel core. I started my search in the cargo hold.

My light danced around the boxes strewn all around the hold as I climbed over and under them. Most of the boxes were helpfully labeled with their contents, but I wasn't interested in bolts of canvas or computer chips. Shrews had chewed through some of the crates of grain and eaten the seeds inside, but Eden base would certainly want the huge spools of wire and the crates of ammunition. I made a mental note of their location.

"I think I have it!" Brent's excited voice called through the dark ship.

I grabbed one of the nearby crates of ammo and hoisted it onto my shoulder, rejoining the group congregating around the closed door.

"Good work, Brent. Primary objective attained," General Carthage said.

Brent held the precious power core in his arms, his light gleaming off the smooth metal cylinder of its casing.

I set the crate of ammunition on the floor and shone my light on the label.

"Excellent, soldier," the General praised. My face warmed at his approval and I was grateful no one could see it in the dark.

"We'll take as much as we can carry now and load up the shuttle when it arrives to pick us up," he continued.

"There's wire and cloth and computer parts up there as well, sir," I reported.

"Good. We'll take an inventory while we wait for transport back to Eden base. We need all the supplies we can get," he added unnecessarily.

"Oh no," Ms. Arnson said softly from nearby. I climbed over to where her light glowed.

"What is it?" I asked her.

"Embryo storage." She crouched down next to an enormous crate that had split open when the transport ship crashed. I recognized the big metal cylinder inside; we had one at Eden base. This one was silent, dependent on power that had not run for three years. The frozen contents must have thawed out and spoiled long ago.

"That's a real shame," I agreed. I knew how valuable each of those little tubes had been. All that DNA wasted. All that diversity for our future destroyed.

Ms. Arnson laid her hand on the still metal side of the container, as if hoping that somehow it would still feel cold, that the embryos inside might somehow be saved. But the surface was as hot as everything else in this stifling hold, and she drew her hand back, disappointed.

"We'll be okay without them. We have plenty at Eden," I tried to reassure her.

"Maybe," she answered. "But it's still sad."

The Horizon ships had only been equipped to carry five hundred people. Not enough genetic diversity for a species to survive. So we'd brought thousands of frozen embryos with us. Some children were "naturals," like Josh. Josh was my dad's real son, conceived naturally when my parents fell in love. A woman's first living child proved she could carry a baby, so the next one was always born of one of the frozen straws of DNA from Earth men long dead. That meant Josh was my half-brother, and our dad wasn't my real father at all. My biological father had been dead for two hundred years, but he'd sent the seed of his DNA to be frozen and shipped across the galaxy. We brought the DNA of thousands of men with us, and frozen embryos from thousands more couples who sent their genes into space, into the future.

A woman's third child comes from one of the precious embryos in storage, so my little sister Malia isn't technically my dad's or my mom's. She was an Earth Child, a pale girl from the time of pure races, a time long gone as we carefully maintained our genetic diversity through generations in space. She looked nothing like us, but we loved her fiercely. I remember how excited I was when she was born, just three years before landing. The memory made it more painful to imagine all these Earth Children who would never be born.

Back at the closed exterior door, the General was giving orders.

"Shiro, Brent, you head aft to the cockpit. See if any of the communications gear can be salvaged. Use your sat trans to plug in and try to get some power flowing. If you can, send a mayday to Eden base and give them our coordinates."

"Aye, General," Brent said, and the two of them disappeared toward the front of the ship.

"Caleb, you stay here with Jack and Sara; check the bandage on Jack's leg. I'm heading back outside to see if I can get any sat signal from on top of the ship."

The door squealed a protest that momentarily silenced the jungle around the ship as the General slipped outside. I held my breath, waiting to hear the familiar hum and chirp of the smaller reptiles pick back up, indicating a small degree of safety. The high-pitched background din began after a minute, and I blew out my cheeks. Night had fallen and only the forest's green phosphorescent glow streamed through the open door. My instincts screamed for me to close it, but if the General wanted it closed, he'd have done it himself. I reassured myself that only T-rex and a few of his large cousins hunted after nightfall, and none of them would be able to fit through the small opening. Still, I kept glancing through it, alert for any movement.

"It's the silence I can't stand, you know?" I said to Jack.

"Yeah, you get really used to the constant noise. You don't even notice it until it's gone," he agreed quietly.

His pale cheeks looked ghostly in the glow of my flashlight. I looked down at his leg. The bandage was soaked, bright red blood flashing through the white wrapping and the danger of his injury finally hit me.

Neither of Jack's parents had survived the first year on Ceti, so Mom had unofficially adopted him into our family a long time ago. And when the General broke the news that my older brother's scouting team had failed to report in, it was Jack who caught my mom as she collapsed, sobbing. Now he was the closest thing to an older brother I'd ever have. I couldn't let anything happen to him.

"So what did Sara find up there?" Jack asked.

"Embryo freezer," I answered. "Listen, I think we need to get your bandage changed, buddy."

"Okay," he said and I stuck my flashlight under my chin to paw through my pack. There was ammunition and a spare charge for my sat transmitter, and my half-full canteen. I had a sparker and a folding knife but nothing I could use for bandages.

"Wait here," I told Jack. "I need to find some first aid stuff."

He didn't reply. Ms. Arnson was rummaging through more boxes toward the stern, and I picked my way over to her.

"Have you seen any medical supplies? We need to get Jack rebandaged," I said.

"Not here. Try over there," she indicated with her flashlight. She was still talking in that strange, clipped, emotionless voice. It unnerved me more than a breakdown would have. She must have been holding her shock and fear inside, but whether she was trying to put up a brave front for us or just mentally denying the position we were in, I wasn't sure.

"Thanks, Ms. Arnson." I wasn't really sure if I should still call her Ms. Arnson. The other guys all just called her Sara. And I was an adult now. But somehow I just couldn't bring myself to use her first name. I wanted to say something more, something adult and soldierly, but the only things that came to mind were stupid.

I was heading in the direction she pointed me when the night fell silent and the ship vibrated slightly. The floor trembled through my boots, and a shiver traveled straight up my spine. Only one 'saur was heavy enough to make the whole ground shake at its step. T-rex, king of the darkness, was heading our way.

CHAPTER 5

An image from one of my favorite movies from Horizon's vaults flashed through my brain, of water in a cup on the dashboard of a car vibrating at the step of a giant predator.

Hardly reassuring.

I crept back toward Ms. Arnson and together we moved Jack farther away from the opening, sitting him down on the floor with his back against the hull's interior wall.

We switched off our flashlights and waited. My ears were so attuned to the usual night noises that the silence echoed inside my skull. Tiny scurrying sounds indicated that whatever variety of shrew had made this ship home had realized danger was approaching. I stifled a scream as one ran across my boot on its way to a safer nest.

Dim light from one of Ceti's moons filtered in through the door, and my eyes adjusted quickly to the gloom. I sucked in a breath when a shadow darkened the open doorway, but it quickly resolved into the shape of the General, who had wisely turned off his own light.

"Did you reach base?" I asked him in a whisper.

"Negative. Too much tree cover. If we can't get the ship's communications working we'll have to find a clearing."

The Rex's footfalls were getting closer, dust sifting through the air as the hold's contents shifted slightly under the tiny quakes. We crouched down next to Jack.

Compared to the 'saurs that went cold at night, humans stood out like stars in a black sky, warm all night long. To a Rex's heat sensors, we were easy prey outside the fence.

Movement in the front of the ship made my heart skip a beat, but it was only Brent and Shiro feeling their way blindly back from the cockpit.

"Report," the General whispered when they found us.

"Negative, General. The cockpit is smashed to bits. We couldn't even get in. This ship is dead." Shiro sounded dejected even in a whisper.

My stomach turned over. We were trapped out here in the black jungle. And the approaching footfalls told us we were already being hunted.

The ship rocked slightly and we smelled the sour scent of the Rex. We all froze and held our breath.

The forest light illuminating the open door was abruptly darkened by an enormous shadow. Ms. Arnson gripped my arm.

The Rex's nostril filled the doorway and sniffed inside. I gagged as it exhaled, filling the small hold with its fetid stench. None of us made a sound.

It sniffed again. They had learned fast what we smelled like. No doubt it knew we were here. Its heat sensors couldn't pick us out inside the warm metal hull, but it could smell us right through the doorway. A bloodsucker bug landed on my face and started to feed. I stayed motionless, barely breathing.

The Rex lifted its head back up and dim light entered the doorway for a moment. I dared to hope it had somehow missed our scent over all the other smells in this ship.

Its shadow fell across the doorway again, and the Rex's front leg thrust through, clawing blindly at us. Its reach was longer than the reach of its real dinosaur namesake, and ended in a three-fingered hand tipped with razor sharp claws.

We threw ourselves backwards, knocking down piles of crates as we scrambled away from the grasping talons. I fell over something sharp and landed hard on my back. Shiro's knee connected with my jaw as he climbed over me in his panic. I tasted blood but felt no pain.

A scream shot through my nerves like an electric current. I sat upright, squinting through the darkness to see who had made that awful sound.

One of the Rex's claws had found Jack propped up against the hull. In our frenzy to get away from the open door, none of us had pulled him to safety. He screamed again as the Rex dragged him toward the opening. I froze, unable to move, unable to think.

A shadow dove out from behind me, the General launching awkwardly toward the screaming soldier. The General grabbed Jack's foot and pulled, starting a deadly tug-of-war between man and 'saur with Jack's body as the rope. But even the General was no match for a Rex. Jack's final scream ended with a gurgle as the Rex's claws punctured through his chest and the Rex dragged his limp form across the transport's floor. My almost-brother disappeared through the doorway in a smear of warm blood.

CHAPTER 6

We huddled in stunned silence.

Jack was gone.

My brother's best friend who'd teased me aboard the Horizon, the first kid to set foot on this hostile planet, was dead. I could hardy get my brain around it.

"Stay down and plug your ears," the General said.

The Rex still crouched outside the transport's open hatch. There was a small clinking sound, then a huge explosion thundered right outside the door. The General had thrown a grenade. I didn't know he had one.

The heavy footfalls vibrated the ship as the angry Rex pounded off into the forest. We stayed frozen on the floor until the night sounds started up again and we knew it was gone.

The General sat up.

"Count off," he said, and we did. I think he said it by habit. We all knew who was missing. I swallowed hard and squinted my eyes against tears that threatened to fall.

We gathered around him, too near the open door for my liking. My lip was starting to swell where Shiro had kneed me in the face while climbing over me. My brain felt numb.

In the three years since we landed on Ceti, I had never been so close to a Rex. I never wanted to be that close again.

"We need to contact Eden," the General said. "By now they know we're missing, but they won't send a rescue shuttle unless they hear from us. We'll find a clearing where we can get a sat signal and then get somewhere safe until they arrive."

"I'll go," Shiro said, and I turned to stare at him.

"We stay together," the General said.

Ms. Arnson spoke quietly. "Rexes travel alone and are very territorial. The one that . . . the one we just saw is probably the only one in the area. It . . . won't be hungry now. So tonight's our best chance to find somewhere to get a signal out and get back in here to wait."

"We could wait for daylight," Brent suggested.

Ms. Arnson shook her head. "At night we just have the Rex to worry about. In daylight there will be Gilas and Wolves, and all the snakes will be active."

"We could just as easily step on a snake in the dark," Brent said. Ceti was home to a wide variety of venomous snakes. Just about every creature on this planet seemed like it had evolved especially to kill us.

The debate seemed to calm Ms. Arnson down. Talking about the native inhabitants of this planet focused her mind and she slipped naturally into teacher mode.

"True," she said, "but at night the big ones will be sleeping in the trees. In daylight the big ones will be hunting. For us."

The General decided the issue.

"We go tonight and we stay together." He pulled his sat trans out of his pocket and touched the screen. It had no way to reach the satellites in orbit through the dense foliage, but the General had downloaded the most current maps of the area before we left Eden, so he had some idea where we were. We crowded around the glow of the small display.

"Our shuttle went down about here," he said, pointing to a dense green area that looked exactly like all the dense green area around it. "So our current position is right around here." He touched another identical patch of green and made note of our location on the trans. "We're only a few kilometers from these hills. There will be some open areas there." He indicated some brown patches of bare rock that looked impossibly far from our current location.

"Will that still be in this Rex's territory?" I asked, trying and failing to keep the tremor out of my voice.

"I have no idea," Ms. Arnson answered. "Their territories extend for kilometers, and who knows if this is the middle or the edge? But I don't see that we have any choice."

"Caleb, you found ammunition in here somewhere?" The General waited for my answer.

"Yes, sir. I'll show you." My voice sounded a little stronger. Just don't think about Jack. You have to get through this on your own.

"Brent, you and Shiro collect anything else you can find in here that you think we can use. Caleb and I will get as much ammo as we can carry. Hopefully there will be weapons, too. Take ten minutes and gather what you can."

We found enough handguns for each of us to get two, a couple of small handheld grenade launchers, plenty of ammunition, and some wickedly long knives. As I strapped one on, I had the thought that if any 'saurs got close enough for me to reach for a knife, it was probably already too late.

I caught myself thinking about movies. Horizon's virtual storage used to hold every book and movie ever written in English, the official language of Horizon Alpha. I devoured books as a kid, partly because I loved reading about how things once were on a planet long destroyed, and partly because recreation was fairly limited, even on such a huge ship. I realized how lucky I was to be born only twelve years before we reached our destination planet. Generations had been born, lived their whole lives, and died without ever setting foot on natural ground. How soul-crushing it must have been for them to know they wouldn't live to see the culmination of this voyage, to find a new home for the tiny portion of humanity that made the journey.

To pass the time, I watched every film we brought on board. Histories, horror, thrillers. But my favorites were the science fiction movies. I loved watching what people thought the future would hold. They imagined us zipping around on jet packs, shooting laser guns at aliens. I watched them so many times their words were burned into my brain.

Since the crash, I often wished the ancient Earth scientists had time to develop laser guns before they shipped us into space. But when the ancients realized Earth's days were numbered, they stopped working on all that stuff. Nothing but Horizon mattered anymore; how it would travel, what we would eat, where we would go. Maybe if Earth had survived, I'd be flying around in a hovercraft shooting a phaser; instead, I found myself on a dinosaur planet armed with guns that were designed two hundred years ago. Now more than ever, I wished that laser guns had been a priority. But they weren't, so we did our best to fight off dinosaurs with handguns.

The General divvied up the weapons.

Ms. Arnson held the pistol he handed her like it was about to bite her. I'd seen her handle a baby Gila she was studying back at Eden like it was the safest thing in the world, even though the tiny creature already held enough venom in its little poison sacs to kill the whole class. But she looked like she'd be more comfortable holding that baby 'saur again instead of a loaded gun. I was thankful for the three years I'd been in Army training while I finished school. At least I knew how to shoot.

We packed up the few medical supplies Shiro and Brent had found, and we each got a canteen. There were some vitamin bars on the ship, but I hoped we'd be back in Eden by lunchtime tomorrow. My stomach growled at the thought.

"Everyone ready?" asked the General. He picked up the heavy pack containing the precious fuel core, our mission objective.

"Ready, sir," we answered.

There was a smear of blood on the door frame where the Rex had dragged Jack through.

"Fly free, Jack Branch," Ms. Arnson murmured as she passed it. I echoed the sentiment, reaching out to touch a finger to the dark stain.

The General led us out into the night.

CHAPTER 7

We turned our flashlights off so our eyes could adjust to the darkness. Flashlights would be a beacon to any Rex in the area, and although the General had scared away the one that killed Jack, we didn't want to press our luck. A pack of wandering humans might be too tempting for another Rex to hesitate leaving its own territory.

It was never completely dark in the forest. Thousands of insects we called skitters gave the forest luminescence at night. They flew up through the canopy by day, where the algae that had symbiotically colonized their bodies absorbed the sunlight. At night, the algae used the light to secrete complex sugars for the skitters to feed on. The waste products the insects produced glows in the dark, so most leaf surfaces were coated with the softly glowing green slime.

Earth had nothing like it, and I sometimes imagined how dark an Earth forest must have been compared to the cool, green light of Eden. The thought of such heavy darkness chilled me. Eden's nighttime glow reminded me of Horizon, constantly bathed in the luminous radiation of its nuclear exhaust. We used the skitters' light now to pick our way through the forest in single file. The slime left faint phosphorescent streaks on our skin where the foliage brushed against us.

The General ordered Ms. Arnson right behind him, and I followed her. Brent and Shiro were last.

We walked for hours, cautiously breaking our trail through the dense underbrush. I didn't realize how tired I was until I walked into the back of Ms. Arnson, who stopped at the General's hand signal.

"Sorry," I whispered.

We gathered behind the General who signaled us to be silent with a finger over his lips. He pointed straight ahead.

I squinted through the dim jungle, not seeing anything unusual. Then the sour tang of 'saur skin hit my nostrils, and I peered deeper into the thick ferns.

A shape resolved before my eyes, a still form curled around the base of a huge tree. I could barely see it, but the dark shadow of its body blocked the phosphorescent foliage in a distinctive shape. It breathed slowly in the chilly air. Gila.

Standing up, its shoulders would be taller than any of us. Its four legs were tucked in under its body to conserve heat. Its round head rested on the moist soil, and its long tail curled most of the way around the tree. The venomous spine on its tail curved in a wicked spike off the tip. Any creature descending from the high branches in the early morning would likely not live to touch the ground.

My lips started to tremble as electric terror shot through me. I saw these creatures through the fence from time to time, but no electric charge separated us today. If it woke up, one of us would die.

Run! Escape! my brain screamed. My feet obeyed. I spun around, poised to sprint through the forest away from the green-scaled predator that slept mere steps away. Shiro must have seen the panic in my eyes because he gripped my shoulders and stared right at me. Neither of us said a word, but the steel of his gaze and the set of his jaw ordered me to be still and silent.

My heart was pounding so loud in my chest I was sure it would wake the sleeping 'saur. Step by step we backed away from the tree. Shiro released me when he was sure I wasn't going to bolt, and my shoulders slumped out of his hands. He didn't say it, but I knew what he was thinking. Josh wouldn't have panicked. Jack wouldn't run.

But Josh and Jack weren't here. There was only Caleb, Josh's cowardly little brother, about to pee his pants on his first mission into the jungle. My face burned with shame in the darkness.

We stopped when the General felt we had reached a safe distance, and huddled together to whisper.

"That was a Gila," Ms. Arnson said, in case anyone hadn't realized that venomous death was sleeping under a tree just a short walk away.

"Won't wake up for a few more hours," the General replied. "We'll be long away. We'll skirt this area in case there are other members of its group around. I had hoped we'd reach the hills by morning, but this will put us behind."

I didn't want to travel by day, but I certainly didn't want to spend another night in the jungle.

"Do we push on?" I asked, not sure what I hoped he'd answer.

"No. We'll find a tree at daybreak and climb."

We turned east and resumed our quiet, furtive trek.

Despite the terror of being beyond the fence's safety, my eyes felt dry and heavy. I sipped water from my canteen. The soreness was seeping in to my shoulders, and the cut on my lip had swelled up. I felt like a baby for thinking it, but I wished we were home. Then I thought about where we were and figured everyone here must wish they were home, too. Even the General couldn't be enjoying this.

✦ ✦ ✦

I didn't notice the jungle starting to lighten in the cool of pre-dawn, but when the General called a halt, I realized I could see up to the canopy where light was filtering through the high treetops. The 'saurs would be waking up soon as the sun's heat warmed their blood. We needed to be somewhere safe.

Brent found a good tree, sturdy and wide with enough low branches for us to start the climb. My pack weighed me down, and the guns on my hips dug into my thighs as I struggled upwards.

I reached overhead for a branch and pulled myself up. A soft hiss stopped me cold.

A yellow snake thicker than my waist lay coiled in the V of the tree branch, disturbed by my weight. Its black eyes were lidless, alien. I froze, halfway up onto the branch where the reptile waited. It stared at me and I couldn't look away, hypnotized by the unblinking black eyes.

In a second the snake disappeared, shoved off its branch by the butt of Shiro's rifle. I heard it crash into the underbrush below.

"Thanks," I said, throwing a shaky leg over the newly-vacated branch.

"No problem," he replied. He smiled and patted my back to reassure me. "First mission is always the hardest."

I snorted. "First mission? You say that like they're all like this?"

He stopped smiling. "No, they aren't all like this. But any time we leave the fence-line there's a risk. How many soldiers have we lost in the three years we've been on this scat-planet?" He shook his head.

I knew about loss. I still had my mom and my little sister Malia, safe behind electric wire at Eden base, but Horizon killed my father the day we entered Ceti's orbit, the jungles of Eden had claimed my brother just three months ago, and I'd lost another brother last night.

I wasn't going to lose anyone else.

CHAPTER 8

I slept fitfully in the tree, waking at every sound, every rustle of breeze that moved the branches where I'd wedged myself in. I had worried that I might roll right out of the tree in my sleep, but that worry—and all my other worries—kept me from sleeping deeply enough to forget where I was.

We took turns keeping watch as the day wore on, but we had climbed high enough into the canopy that we couldn't see to the distant ground below. Lots of the smaller 'saurs could climb trees, but a little zap with a lightning stick sent the little ones scurrying away. As long as the charges held on the sticks, we had little to fear in the high canopy. But we couldn't stay here forever.

I took a portion of the day watch. An afternoon rainstorm

pelted into the canopy above us. The leaves blocked the raindrops' fall, and the branches filled with wet mist. I strained to see through the foliage, alert for any large movements below that would signal danger near our tree, but only the normal sounds of the jungle met my ears.

Brent had the final watch before the sun set and we resumed our journey. After waking him up, I curled back up in the V of the tree and tried to rest as best I could.

The rain had stopped by the time I awoke. The bits of sky I could see through the treetops were purple, and stars were coming into view when the General roused us all. He led the climb down and we paused near the bottom of the tree for him to toss down some smaller branches he'd broken off to make sure no camouflaged 'saurs were waiting down there. No Gila curled around the trunk, and we dropped silently to the damp forest floor.

I had no idea how he knew where we were. Without the sunset to guide me, I was lost. But he started off confidently and we dropped into file behind him, in the same order as last night.

They put me in the middle so I won't bolt. My feet were heavy in my wet boots.

I hoped we'd reach the mountains tonight. The thought of spending another night huddled in a treetop made my shoulders ache.

We stopped to split up some of the rations we'd brought from the downed transport. Some of the packaged food that had left Earth on Horizon two hundred years ago was still edible. Vacuum-packed protein bars tasted like nothing at all after their long trip through space, but at least they'd been sealed away from the little shrews that infested the crashed ship. Each of us ate a bar and drank from our canteens as we walked.

Shiro and Brent murmured behind me.

"How long will it take to get a shuttle out to us?" Brent asked.

Shiro answered, "Maybe an hour or two. Depends where we are and how easy it will be to land one."

Brent grunted. "Bronton was our best pilot."

"He was," Shiro agreed. "But McCarthy will do fine. Don't worry."

"I'm not worried," Brent said. The tremor in his voice revealed that was a lie.

I'm worried, I thought, but didn't say it. They already knew.

In fits and starts, we made our way through the jungle. I lost count of how many times we stopped, holding our breath as we peered through the darkness to see what had made the General halt. Sometimes we would backtrack or change our course, and other times we waited tense moments before cautiously resuming our journey. The chirping songs of the smaller reptiles reassured us, but overconfidence on Ceti equaled a quick, bloody death, and we remained on high alert.

We stopped to fill our canteens when we came across a shallow stream. My boots soaked through in seconds and the chill of the water seeped into my skin.

Spotting an old rotted log resting on the bank, I set my canteen down and plopped onto it. The soft wood gave way beneath me and my legs flew up as my body plunged backwards into the collapsing seat.

"Oh, gross, what's that smell?" I muttered, pulling myself up out of the remains of the moist log. "Nasty rotten wood."

Ms. Arnson looked as if she were going to smile, but then froze and cocked her head to the side. "Do you hear something?"

The hairs on the back of my neck stood up as my ears registered a faint noise, a high-pitched whine whose direction I couldn't place.

She grabbed her pack from the ground and darted over to where I was trying to brush off my butt, sticky from the inside of the wet log.

"What did you do?" she murmured.

I pulled my hand up to my nose and sniffed the goo that was soaking into my pants. It smelled sour.

Not like rot.

Like 'saur.

"It's a nest," Ms. Arnson said.

We peered into the cavity within the hollow log that I'd crashed through. A small clutch of tiny intact eggs surrounded a pile of broken, sticky shards, their beige shells crushed. Some of those shards were sticking out of my pants and I rubbed harder, trying to clean the goo off myself.

"I didn't mean it," I said. "What kind of 'saur lays eggs in a log?"

Ms. Arnson looked up, the high-pitched whine coming from all around us now. She looked at me and we both spoke at the same time.

"Buzzers!"

The air around us exploded with noise and movement. Fist-sized, winged 'saurs dive-bombed our party from all sides. Tiny, sharp-toothed mouths punctured our exposed flesh.

"What the . . ." the General sputtered. "Why are they attacking?"

I batted at the swarm, feeling small trickles of blood running down my face. "I . . . I sat on their nest," I panted.

"Everybody move!"

I grabbed my canteen from the ground and swung it around me as I ran. We splashed upstream as the Buzzers bounced off us, taking mouthfuls of our skin and clothing with them. Their wings were delicate enough that a direct hit from my canteen sent them crashing into the stream, but there were hundreds of them, an enraged cloud of bloody teeth and talons.

"Take your pants off!" Ms. Arnson panted, running next to me. Streaks of blood made her blond hair mostly pink.

"What?" I stopped running and batted at the swarm.

"Your pants," she repeated. "They smell their eggs on your pants. You have to wash them off."

The rest of the squad heard her and ran back to cluster around me. They waved their lightning sticks in the air, filling the stream with the smell of charred Buzzer as the little fliers got zapped in flight.

I dropped to a crouch in the middle of the circle and unzipped my pants. Facing away from Ms. Arnson, I pulled them down and over my soaked boots, rubbing them frantically against the rocks in the stream. The smell had seeped into my underwear. I'm only going so far. I sat down in the stream in my underpants and scooted across the rocks, my face burning as much with shame as with the hundred little bites.

Finally the swarm dissipated. A few angry holdouts still circled, sizzling as Shiro or Brent found them with the lightning sticks.

I wrung out my pants and pulled them on. "Sorry," I said.

The General glared at me. Brent and Shiro knelt down in the stream to start washing the blood from their faces and arms.

Ms. Arnson crouched next to me. "Are you okay?"

"Yeah," I said, turning away from her.

"We need to wash off all the blood. Another 'saur might smell it."

"I know."

Shiro ambled over as I washed my exposed skin. "You okay, Squirt?" It was my brother's old nickname for me and it rankled even as it brought a lump to my throat.

"I'm fine."

"That's a novel approach," he said, patting me on the back. "Squash the eggs before the 'saurs can hatch. I like it, but I don't think there's enough of us to clear all the 'saurs off the planet."

I shook my head, too embarrassed to answer.

"But honestly," he continued, "I think I could have gone my whole life without seeing you in your underpants flopping around in the water. That's going to haunt my nightmares." He grinned and my tense shoulders relaxed a little.

The General squatted down next to me. "Everybody smear up with mud. Cover up all these fresh wounds."

I was close enough to my fellow soldiers that I could tell that we all smelled ripe in the sweaty jungle. Now we were all bloody. Our scent trail would be easy for a Wolf pack to follow if they came upon it tomorrow. We splashed up the stream in hope of confusing any predators that might hunt us in daylight.

Soon we would leave the dense jungle and get a sat signal.

Then all we had to do was wait for the shuttle and fly home.

★ ★ ★

We left the stream and headed up the steeper slope. More moonlight penetrated through the moist forest as it gave way to a drier, rockier hillside. My heart lightened a bit as we climbed out into open air. The oppressive sweltering jungle felt like a heavy coat around my shoulders, and I was glad to shrug it off. There were dangers in the dry rocks as well, but most of the creatures that dwelled in the higher elevations were smaller than humans and kept away from us if they could. An unlucky step on a rock snake could be fatal, but we shuffled ahead, enjoying the improved visibility of the night.

The General herded us under a rocky overhang and told us to wait for him there. He left the backpack containing the power core and climbed higher on the hillside hoping to pick up the sat signal. The satellites weren't always in the right place to pick up our frequency even if we had a clear view of the sky.

We sat on the dry ground while the General made the call back to base. The wind up here ruffled my hair and blew dusty grit into my eyes. I closed them and leaned back against the cool stones. I didn't mean to fall asleep, but the last two nights of fear caught up with me, and I must have dozed off.

I woke up to the sound of the General yelling at someone. Sitting bolt upright, I looked around to see where the rest of the team was. Ms. Arnson was asleep nearby, and Shiro was keeping watch. The General must have been arguing with Brent, but I couldn't see either one of them.

The rock I was leaning on had dug into my back and it took me a few seconds to straighten up. I brushed dry mud off my itchy neck and shook the dirty bits out of my shirt. The General's voice stopped me cold.

"They're not coming. We're on our own."

CHAPTER 9

"What do you mean, they're not coming, sir?" Shiro asked. His high-pitched voice was shrill in the wind.

"Everyone huddle up." Ms. Arnson struggled slowly to her feet and leaned against the wall. She looked as tired as I felt. The General herded us behind the sheltering rock face.

"Eden base had a power failure last night," the General began and my stomach clenched. My mother and sister were at base. They were all I had left. "Brachis shorted out the fence-line and the power core overloaded. They've had to hook up the two remaining shuttles to keep the fence juiced. If they send one of the shuttles for us, they won't have enough power to run the fences."

We all knew what that would mean.

"What about the hydro turbines?" I asked. My heart was starting to pound. They have to come for us. They just have to.

"I'm sure they're working on them. But they're not operational right now, either. The two shuttles are all that's keeping Eden powered. I'm sure you understand. They can't risk the whole base just to come get us."

"But we have another power core," Shiro said. "If they'd just fly out here, we could have it hooked up in a couple of hours. That's why we came on this scatting mission in the first place."

The General shook his head. "Too risky. I told them how our shuttle went down. If they did send us rescue and we lost that shuttle too, that would be it for Eden. They can't risk it. They'll get a week or two out of the shuttles' power, and maybe that will give them time to figure something out."

"They haven't figured it out in three years." I regretted the words as soon as I said them. Everyone at Eden base worked tirelessly to keep it safe. But nothing they came up with ever worked for long. This cursed planet was at war with the humans who were trying to survive its hostility, and the humans weren't winning.

"We have no choice here." The General didn't sound angry anymore. His shoulders sagged, which scared me almost as much as anything else since the pterosaur clipped our shuttle in the air. A Rex up close was terrifying. The General giving up hope would be worse.

He looked out over the dark forest. "We'll have to walk home."

"But we're kilometers away from base, sir. We'll never make it back." Brent said. The silence that followed showed we were all thinking the same thing.

Ms. Arnson's voice sounded deceptively calm. "We made it this far. We'll travel at night and sleep in the trees. The General is right. We have no choice. We've got to get this power core back to Eden."

"We're about a hundred kilometers out from Eden now. If we

push hard, we can make it back in about five days, walking." The General made it sound easy, like all we had to do was walk the distance. Like every 'saur in this part of Ceti wouldn't be sniffing our trail. Like he really thought any of us were going to make it back alive.

"Can we stay up in the hills?" I sounded whiny and afraid. Ms. Arnson patted me on the back to reassure me, and that just made me mad.

"These hills make a U shape that arcs away from where we're going. We'll cross near them again about halfway back, but if we stick to the hills we'll add over a week to the trip. Eden has maybe two weeks' power left. Less if anything touches the fence and causes a surge."

"But it would be so much safer going," Brent said.

Yes, Brent, I thought. Convince him to stay up in the hills.

"Safer for us," the General agreed. "But not completely safe, and not worth the time it would take. Wolves hunt in the foothills, and if a Rex sees us, it won't hesitate to leave the jungle. We could spend an extra week walking and still not make it back."

"I agree with the General," Ms. Arnson said. "Eden's only hope is for us to get this core back as fast as we can. We need to start back tonight."

So it was decided. We all looked at the maps on our sat transmitters, orienting ourselves to our location, the hills we were on now, and Eden's location. It looked impossibly far away.

Brent picked up the heavy power core and the General took a lighter bag of supplies. The General motioned for me to join him and we moved a little away from the group as they collected the small amount of gear that would somehow have to get us safely back home.

"I spoke to your mother." I looked down at my boots. The General continued. "I told her you were with me and I promised her I'd keep you safe. Stay close to me. We're going to get back to her. I promise."

I nodded and returned to the rest of the team.

I checked my pistols and ammunition. I was carrying about

fifty rounds, which had seemed like a lot when I packed them up at the transport but now felt laughably inadequate. Fifty rounds against a Rex. Fifty rounds against a Gila. Or a pack of Wolves.

Crazy, terrified laughter bubbled up from somewhere inside me, and I bit my lip to keep it from coming out. If I started laughing, I might never stop. A small gurgle escaped my lips as I fought the panic that threatened to unhinge me.

"Five people, a hundred kilometers, and a thousand 'saurs that want to eat us. What could possibly go wrong?" I wondered.

"Not now, Caleb," Brent snapped.

"Quiet," the General commanded, and we both fell silent.

The General divided the rest of the food among us and made sure we each had weapons in easy reach. He said it was in case we got separated somehow, but we all knew he was sharing out what we had because he didn't think we'd all make it back. Like the scientists of Earth had packed humans into four Horizon ships, four Arks to carry human refugees away from a doomed planet, the General was hedging his bets. Maybe he was right. Maybe some of us would make it back to Eden alive.

As we hiked back down the hillside and entered the steaming jungle, I followed him closely. His shoulders still sagged under the weight of his pack, and I understood that even our leader didn't believe any of us would live to see Eden again.

CHAPTER 10

We pushed through the thick undergrowth, smeared brown and green with mud and skitter slime. In another hour, dawn would make us head up a tree for safety, and the General wanted to cover as much ground as we could. We spoke in whispers and jumped at every breaking twig.

"We should have stayed in the hills." Brent's voice from behind me wouldn't carry up to the General leading us.

"It's not just about us. We have to make time." Shiro answered him just as softly.

"But it's all for nothing if we get killed out here," Brent said.

"It's all for nothing anyway," I said. I couldn't see the other soldiers' faces in the pre-dawn darkness but I heard Shiro sigh behind me.

"It's not for nothing. This core will keep Eden going for a while longer."

"How long?" I demanded, looking back over my shoulder at him. I could almost make out his expression. He was looking down at the ground, maybe sorry he'd said anything at all. I kept talking, as much to myself as to him. "A few months? A year? We've been here three years and it all comes down to one stupid power core?"

Ms. Arnson spoke up from in front of me. There was no way the General couldn't hear this exchange now.

"We just need to buy them some more time. The engineers will get the hydroelectric or the wind turbines going. Then we won't need power cores."

I pretended to accept what she said, but whether it was the exhaustion of the past two days' walking or the stress of near-constant terror, I was having a hard time caring right now. If we made it back with the core, would it matter? In another year, would there be a single human left alive on this planet?

The subtle vibration of the soft ground under my boots snapped me out of my reverie. We all stopped in our tracks.

Again I felt it. The smallest buzz of the damp soil concussed by a very heavy footfall.

We looked wildly around us, unsure which direction the Rex was coming from. The vibrations were coming harder and faster now. It was getting closer.

"Up, now!" the General hissed and we each bolted for the nearest tree.

I stuffed my pistol into the back waistband of my pants and climbed for my life. I was making a lot of noise, but there was nothing I could do about that. Get higher. Get out of reach. My palms scraped on the damp bark and my tired thighs protested each step. I didn't look down, only up, higher, safer.

When I was high enough to see the sun's earliest rays peeking through the foliage, I paused, panting. I peered out through the branches. From the south came the unmistakable commotion of a Rex on the move, smaller trees swaying and cracking in the sudden silence as every smaller lizard went still.

Its massive head burst into view, turning left and right to scan the jungle floor. A muffled cry sounded below me and I gripped the nearest branch.

Ms. Arnson was stuck too low on the tree. She clung to the opposite side of the trunk from the Rex. It couldn't see her from where it was right now.

My hands shook on the branch. My brain whirled with indecision. If I climbed down, could I reach her in time? Could I help her up higher to safety? Or were we better off staying still and silent, hoping the Rex wouldn't notice our scent? I bit my lower lip. What would Josh have done if he were here?

The Rex sniffed the air, surely noticing our unusually potent scent. This far from Eden base it might not have smelled humans before, but it certainly could tell there was something warm in these trees.

Ms. Arnson looked up and her eyes locked with mine.

Be silent. Don't move, I willed her with my gaze. Her mouth was open a little bit and her eyes looked shiny. The sight of her abject terror made me feel braver somehow. I risked a small gesture, pointing around the tree to where I could see the Rex, and then motioning her to stay where she was. I couldn't tell if she understood me, but she remained frozen in place.

After an eternity, the Rex moved. I pressed my body into the tree trunk as the whole forest shook in the wake of the huge 'saur's passing. It crashed away through the forest and I held my breath until the usual songs of the smaller lizards started up again. I sagged into the tree.

CHAPTER 11

I climbed down the tree until I reached Ms. Arnson and helped her up to a safer spot. We were the only two who had fled up this particular tree, but the General called from nearby and we risked a quick count off. Everyone's voice sounded about as high as we were in the trees, and no one was missing.

Ms. Arnson and I shared a protein pack from my supplies. I tied her to a thick branch for safety, then roped myself to another. Tension hung thick in the air.

"So . . . that went all right," I said. "Better than the last Rex."

She gave me a tight-lipped smile.

I tried to sleep but was too keyed up. Ms. Arnson fidgeted on a branch right below me. She didn't seem sleepy either.

"So why did you come out here?" I asked her after a few minutes.

"Collecting samples," she answered. "The more we can learn about this place, the better. We're stuck here now and we know so little about it."

"You have lots of eggs and plants and stuff back at base." Her makeshift science lab was full of the planet's flora and fauna. Leaves and flowers dried in the sun, open notebooks were full of carefully drawn replicas of everything we had encountered here. Scouting missions had brought her back eggs of every size, and some of them had hatched under her careful incubation. It seemed unlikely that we would ever be able to domesticate any of the 'saurs, but a few of Ms. Arnson's hatchlings had started off well. It broke her heart when they died, lacking some nutrient or parental care she couldn't reproduce. She dissected them with reverence and contributed to our deepening understanding of Eden's inhabitants. Not that it did us much good. Understanding what kind of digestive system a baby Gila had didn't help us at all when Gila poison stung a soldier in the field. Ms. Arnson hoped to figure out an antivenin of some kind, but without the tons of medial and lab equipment that was still orbiting uselessly on the dead Horizon, she was at a disadvantage.

"I wanted to pick up my own. I've asked the units going out to get me things, certain plants and things I wanted. But it's never their main objective and they always come back with the wrong stuff. The General started taking me out on some of the quicker, safer missions last year."

I snorted at that. "Quicker" and "safer" were two words no one would ever use to describe our current mission.

"I didn't think they'd let a female outside the fence." It sounded cruel to say, but it was true. The breeding-age women of Eden were humanity's last hope. They were much too valuable to risk in the army. Our birth rate was supposed to grow exponentially once we left the confines of Horizon and had a whole planet to populate. But few babies had been born since we landed as most of the women hesitated to bring a new life into such a perilous existence.

"I can't have babies, so I'm expendable. Just like you." That last was supposed to be a joke but I heard the pain in her words.

"You can't have a baby?" I repeated. I was glad for the darkness of the night. I couldn't read her expression in the dim glow of the forest. I didn't mean to hurt her feelings, but it surprised me.

"No. Something's wrong with me. The doctors on Earth probably could have fixed it, but not here. I lost two on board Horizon, both of them so early that nobody but me knew I was pregnant. I would have had the ship docs try to figure it out, but then we got here and lost most of the equipment, and most of our doctors, too."

"I'm sorry about the babies," I said. It sounded inadequate, but Ms. Arnson turned and smiled at me.

"It's okay. In a strange way, it's probably for the best. I'd be terrified every minute if I had little ones on this planet. I couldn't imagine how much that must hurt, to lose a son or daughter like that."

She didn't say what "like that" meant, but I knew she meant like Jack and our pilot. Like the other soldiers we'd lost in the shuttle crash.

"I know my mom worries all the time. She cried for a month when Josh didn't come back."

"That must have been awful." She slapped at a bloodsucker on her arm. We were smeared with creek mud, but the buzzing insects found our skin through the cracks.

"Yeah. It was pretty awful." I hadn't meant for this conversation to come around to Josh. That wound was still too open, too fresh. I wasn't ready to talk about my brother yet.

"Maybe if we ever find somewhere safe, my mom can figure out what's wrong with you," I suggested.

"I'd like that. Finding somewhere safe enough for my reproductive cycle to be a priority." She laughed softly. "In the meantime, I have plenty of kids. I teach every child in Eden."

We fell into silence. The air warmed quickly, and I drifted into another day's fitful sleep.

✦ ✦ ✦

We all climbed down and reassembled at dusk. There was still enough light to see some ripe berries on a nearby bush and we all ate as many as we could. We wiped our stained fingers on our pants, leaving dark red streaks. My canteen was nearly empty.

The General led us on through the night. Sometime after midnight, we started to hear the sound of rushing water growing louder as we plodded through the dense underbrush. The sky lightened up ahead and we stopped at the edge of a fast moving river. It was wide enough to cut a swath through the treetop canopy and the glow of Ceti's biggest moon glinted off the splashing drops. The General looked intently up and down the river but said nothing.

After a long pause, Shiro spoke up. "Do we cross, sir?"

The General was holding his arm out as far as he could over the water's edge, trying to get a sat signal without success. Did he know where we were? This river was large enough to show up on a satellite map, but I didn't remember every detail of the path he had chosen when we last saw the terrain up on the hillside.

"We're too far south," the General murmured. I wasn't sure if he meant for us to hear him. "We've swung off course. We shouldn't have come across this branch of the river at all."

"So do we cross?" Shiro persisted, looking over his shoulder through the trees. We all felt exposed on this open riverbank. My hand sweated on the metal of my pistol.

"If we cross once, we'll have to cross back over it to get to Eden," the General seemed to be working out a mental map. "We should have stayed north of this whole tributary. It loops around south of base. I meant for us to stay on the north side of it the whole way."

"It doesn't look very deep. We could wade across it," suggested Brent.

"Here, yes, we could," the General agreed. "But how deep does it get later on? It dumps into our river eventually, and we all know what lives in there."

Actually, we didn't know.

The deep, fast moving water ran close enough to Eden base

that we'd all seen midsize 'saurs taking a drink from its edge. Sometimes a huge gray shadow would leap up out of the dark water and drag a 'saur under before it could turn to run away. Whatever lived in the water had a head the size of a Rex's and the speed of a Wolf. No one really wanted to see any more of it than the flash of yellow teeth and the spray of blood that flowed away into the water.

We filled our canteens and splashed water on our faces one at a time. Nothing lunged out of the water and we all breathed easier once we backed away from its edge and the forest closed around us again.

We kept the river on our left, trudging along in silence. The General held up a hand signaling a stop, and we all raised our weapons.

A wide path opened across our way, a much-used game trail trampled down by herds of 'saurs. They must use this path to drink from the river.

A loud crash sounded too close for comfort, so we dove for the bushes. Shiro jumped down right behind me and clamped his hand over my upper arm. He pulled me close to him and I could hear him breathing. He smelled like old sweat.

Whatever was coming down the game trail was making too much noise to be a Rex. Legs the width of tree trunks stomped into view and I relaxed.

It was Brachis. A whole family of them ambled single file down the game path toward the river. Unlike brachiosaurs from Earth's textbooks, their necks were shorter and their heads larger, but they walked on four legs and ate only plants, stripping whole trees bare as they browsed through the forest.

The female led. Enough moonlight filtered through the trees for me to see her bluish-green hide, scaled and smooth. Three young ones followed her, dappled green and brown, and the huge male brought up the rear. His bright eyes scanned the forest around his family. A whole Wolf pack could take down an adult Brachi, and a Rex could snap their necks with one crunch of its jaws, but the male knew he wouldn't be the subject of any attack.

Any predator that targeted his family would be after the young ones.

We squatted in the bushes, inhaling the sour smell of their huge bodies. No one moved for at least five agonizing minutes after the male's huge tail swept out of sight. We hid and waited, making sure no carnivores were tracking the Brachis. On the General's signal we rose to our feet and dashed across the game trail, crouching low.

I rubbed my arm as we continued our trek. My arm felt bruised where Shiro had gripped me. Making sure I didn't bolt and run. My face burned with embarrassment. I hadn't panicked, hadn't bolted, but Shiro had assumed I would. Had Brent jumped on Ms. Arnson the same way? Or was it just me, just rookie Caleb who couldn't be trusted not to freak out and get us all killed? I hoisted my pack higher on my shoulder and shuffled on.

CHAPTER 12

The river curved in front of us and the General stopped, shaking his head.

"It shouldn't be turning like this. We should be coming around the side of it to track it to the southwest."

I slapped a huge bloodsucker bug off my neck and my hand came away bloody. I wiped it on my shirt and scratched the new bite. My empty stomach twisted sourly.

We were lost.

I had been so sure the General knew where we were going, I had never considered we might get lost out here. How far off course were we? How much time had we added to the trip? Brent swung the pack holding the heavy power core off his shoulders, setting it on the soft ground.

"Maybe it's just a smaller branch or something. Maybe we just need to cross it here and follow it around," he suggested.

"Maybe. But we're scats if we're wrong." The General didn't swear much. It wasn't reassuring to hear it now.

"I can climb out and maybe get a fix on the satellite," Shiro suggested, pointing across the river. A huge tree leaned out across the water, probably knocked down by the tail of some huge 'saur. It had been dead long enough for most of the leaves to fall off. Clear moonlight shone down on the empty branches.

"You stay here and stay together. I'll go," the General began, but Shiro cut him off.

"I'm the best climber, sir. I can get out there the fastest and get us back on track."

The General looked like he wanted to argue, but it was true. Shiro was a great climber. He was fast and light. Josh used to tell us about training with him. My brother would laugh and say Shiro was the only person keeping him from being top of his class. Shiro had taken the news of Josh's death stoically, but the next day there was a fist-sized hole in the wooden wall of the new lookout tower, and he showed up to training with two broken knuckles on his right hand.

"All right," the General agreed. "Be quick about it. Get our position and mark our path. Call into base and let them know our location."

Each soldier had a sat trans in his pack, for all the good they did us in the thick jungle. Shiro checked the battery on his unit and headed off toward the uprooted base of the dead tree.

He clambered up the branches to the thick trunk and climbed out over the river. His trans lit up when it reached the satellite.

Ms. Arnson murmured, "He's got a signal," and everyone turned to look. Shiro stood there for a few minutes, talking too quietly for us to hear. Eden base would be shocked to hear from us. They've gotta figure we're dead by now. I smiled a little, picturing my mom's face when she got the news that for now, at least, we were still alive, still headed home.

The light winked out on his trans unit as he climbed back toward the riverbank. A high-pitched shriek split the night, some 'saur meeting a swift demise. All our heads whipped around toward the sound, including Shiro's. The sudden movement made his foot slip on the damp tree trunk and he fell ten feet to the ground.

A few steps earlier and he'd have landed in the water, cushioning his landing. Or a few steps later and he'd have been over soft mud. But the snap of bone echoed like the cracking of a small twig. Shiro muffled a cry, a single exclamation as he landed on a hard rock sticking up out of the river's edge.

We all broke cover and ran to him.

He pushed himself up onto his elbows, gritting his teeth as we approached. His left leg stuck out in front of him but the right bent back at an unnatural angle.

"Oh, stars, no," Ms. Arnson muttered, crouching next to the fallen soldier.

"I'm okay," he said through clenched teeth. "Just help me up."

He tried to pull himself up on the rock and fell back, grunting in pain when his broken right leg bent underneath him.

"Hold still. We need to get it immobilized." The General pulled a pale roll of bandaging cloth out of his pack. "Caleb, find two strong branches we can use to splint the leg."

I darted into the trees, pulling out my knife. It was serrated on one edge and I sawed through a small branch, stripping off the leaves. I handed Brent the first branch while I stripped another one, which I carried back to the riverbank where pale Shiro sat.

He stifled a scream when the General pulled his broken leg out straight and laid the branches down each side. He bound Shiro's leg tight to the wood from his boot all the way up to his thigh. Shiro moaned softly with each knot of cloth.

I looked away from the white bandages on his leg. Too much like Jack. Way too soon.

"Okay, son, let's see what you can do on it." The General and Brent each took an arm and lifted Shiro to his feet. They pulled his arms over their shoulders, standing three across.

Shiro shuffled his good leg forward and made a small hop, leaning heavily on the men who supported him. He slid the splinted leg under him and tested its strength.

"Scat it!" he grunted, too loud over the noise of the river.

General Carthage and Brent grabbed his waist as he collapsed, easing him back onto the softer ground.

"It's no good, sir," Shiro said weakly. "I can't walk."

"Then we'll make a sledge and drag you." The General turned toward the trees and took a step before Shiro's quiet voice called him back.

"I'll slow you down. You'll never make it dragging me along. You'll all die because of me. You have to go on."

The General didn't speak. He stood silent for a moment, staring out across the dark river. His shoulders slumped as he knelt down in the mud next to the young soldier and put his hand on Shiro's shoulder.

"Never thought I'd go out like this, sir." Shiro's voice sounded stronger, more certain. "Figured I'd get eaten by a Rex, swallowed by a river monster . . . didn't think I'd slip off a tree."

"We won't leave a man down," the General insisted.

"You have to. You know it, sir." Shiro said it kindly.

Ms. Arnson turned away from the group. She struggled against tears, her breathing ragged.

"I can stay with him, sir," Brent said. "You go on and send help back from base."

"Negative. I won't leave two behind." The General's eyes were downcast. Maybe he wouldn't leave two. But he was going to have to leave one.

"Help me back up onto the tree," Shiro said. "I can crawl back out over the water and talk to Eden by satellite. It's the safest place for me. I can hold out for a few days, maybe long enough for you to send me a shuttle."

I couldn't tell from his face if he really had hope that we might somehow win through and send rescue or if he just said it so we wouldn't feel so guilty for leaving him. He and the General conferred for a few minutes, loading the map from Shiro's trans onto the General's. We weren't too far off course. If we had just followed the river for another kilometer, we'd have made the turn and known where we were. I shivered, picturing Shiro alone here in the jungle, crippled and afraid. How could we leave him here to die? But what else could we do? We couldn't carry him.

He was right. If we didn't leave him, we'd all die with him.

"Hang on, son. We'll send a shuttle just as quick as we can." The General filled Shiro's canteen and packed some food into the lightest backpack.

We helped him stand and boosted him up into the branches where he pulled himself along, sliding on his belly out over the water. The rest of us walked away from the dead tree, leaving our bravest soldier to his lonely fate. I lingered, watching his painful progress. He turned back and our eyes met. He gave an encouraging little wave, a small gesture shooing me away toward the retreating figures entering the forest. He smiled as if to say, Go on, I'll be all right. I wasn't fooled. Shiro was going to die here, alone over the rushing water.

The General and Brent were walking ahead with Ms. Arnson between them. She was still crying softly when I caught up to them. I turned back to catch one last glimpse of Shiro as we rounded the bend in the river. His sat trans was lit up in the open air above the water. I stared for a moment, watching the blue flickering light, a lonely beacon in the night.

"Caleb, come on," Brent murmured from up ahead.

I took a few steps toward the rest of the group and turned back one last time, but Shiro's trans had gone dark.

CHAPTER 13

My eyes burned and I blinked back tears. How were we walking away from one of our own? I bit my lip, plodding after Brent. It could have been me. I was a good climber. I could have crawled out across the tree. If I had, I'd be sitting there now, alone in the forest, waiting for a rescue that had very little chance of getting back in time to save me. Scat it, Shiro. We're coming back for you. Shiro hadn't cried for his own fate, and I wouldn't either. But my throat was full and my vision blurred as I followed the three other surviving members of this decimated team, Eden's last hope, carrying the reactor core through the dark jungle.

The General looked back and saw me scuffling down the path. His eyes lifted and he squinted back through the trees, looking for one last glimpse of Shiro's trans light in the darkness. I watched his face as he searched the night, and I held his gaze when he focused on me.

"We'll be all right, son," was all he said, and the word "son" didn't grate on me the way it usually did.

We camped in the trees again, four of us together in the high branches of a great old hardwood. First watch was the easiest, and the General gave it to Ms. Arnson. We tied ourselves to the branches, but by now my cramped body was getting used to sleeping in the craws with my arms dangling over. I longed for the luxury of sleeping on a flat surface. Somewhere safe behind electric wire.

I woke to the smell of 'saur and reached for my knife, but Ms. Arnson shook her head and pointed at the tall domed heads of some herbivore I didn't recognize. Dappled sunlight glistened off moist scales of bright blue as the creatures browsed the leaves of our tree. We sat still, watching them from above as they ambled through the forest. Their unhurried forage reassured me that no carnivores were hunting nearby, and I relaxed a bit, laying my head against my shoulder.

I was supposed to take the final watch, but since I was already awake I decided to serve my time now and let Brent and the General sleep.

"Sweet dreams," I whispered to Ms. Arnson, and she gave a halfhearted laugh.

"Not likely."

The morning heated up toward noon as I watched the jungle below us through heavy-lidded eyes. A shrill cry echoed through the trees, and my heartbeat quickened as the day suddenly fell silent.

I couldn't see the ground from my vantage point, but I drew my pistol and checked my ammunition. The sound of gunfire was a sure way to attract any predators that had smelled humans before, so we only fired under grave duress. But it felt good to hold the cool metal in my hand as I peered down through the leaves.

Movement on the forest floor made me tighten my grip on the weapon. A dull gray body darted beneath our tree, too fast for a good look. It was followed by another, and another, a single file of shadows moving silently along.

Code W.

Wolves.

They were dinosaurs like all the rest, but what they lacked in bright colors or huge size they made up for in intelligence and communication. Long, stealthy gray bodies were covered from nose to tail with bony plate armor. Chest high to a man, Wolves prowled on four legs, silent and lethal. Someone had compared their pack-hunter style to the wolves of Earth, and the name had stuck. They trotted along with their snaky heads to the ground, sniffing for scent trails to follow. They made complicated clicks deep in their throats which must be a primitive language of some sort, one we had yet to decipher in our limited studies. Earth paleontologists never found anything like them in the ancient rock strata of our lost homeworld. Wolves were pure Eden. And pure death to any prey they chose.

I held my breath as they passed by. Humans were an easy meal for a Wolf pack. Even armed, we were no match for them. Their serrated teeth could cut through a 'saur's tough hide in one bite. Our soft skin must have tasted like candy when they discovered us. They would surround their prey and attack from all sides on a signal from the leader. In our three years here, they had been observed killing everything from the smallest lizards and snakes to the largest Brachis.

The last Wolf in the pack paused at the base of our tree. Its sides heaved as it smelled the leaf litter where we had climbed up here to safety. I couldn't see its eyes, but it clicked twice, a questioning sound as it sniffed. An answering click from the leader sent it loping off without a backward glance, and I sighed. This pack must have never smelled humans before, or they would have recognized our scent and latched onto the easy prey. Wolves couldn't climb, but we would never have gotten out of this tree alive if they had set up an ambush for us on the ground.

The sounds of the forest began again after the pack was out of sight. I holstered my pistol and leaned back against the rough tree bark.

It was time for Brent's watch, so I woke him and settled in to sleep. I dreamed of gray bodies slinking through the branches, sniffing the air and clicking a warning.

CHAPTER 14

Brent woke us up as dusk fell. Ms. Arnson looked like she hadn't slept a bit. This jungle was no place for a naturalist. Had the General had any suspicion of the dangers of this trip, he never would have brought her here. Then again, he wouldn't have brought me, either.

The mission should have taken less than an hour on the ground. A party of eleven, well-armed and well-trained, in Eden's fastest remaining shuttle. It should have been simple to find the power core, load it up, and fly home. But Ceti had a way of turning simple into complicated, and complicated into dead.

Our rations were running low. We had some protein bars in each of our packs, and enough canteens. There were plenty of flowing streams to fill them, but without water purifying tablets we were taking more risk with every drink. Sick soldiers would rapidly become dead soldiers out here on our own.

The maps we all carried on our sat trans still worked, even though we couldn't locate the satellites in the heavy tree cover. Eden base was due west of the bend in the river, the bend Shiro had gone up the tree looking for. The bend that was so close, but would probably cost Shiro his life.

There wasn't much to see in this part of the world. I could trace the cut of the river through the forest, and I could see the mottled green and brown of a huge patch of land just north of the river, close to where we must have been. The barren hills reflected light brown and gray, mostly devoid of foliage kilometers away to the north. We plodded on through the shadows.

"Just another couple of days' walking," Brent muttered from behind me. The General led as usual, followed by Ms. Arnson and me. Now that Shiro was gone, Brent was our rear guard. Could have been worse. The General could have put me right behind him. At least he trusts me enough to have Ms. Arnson between us.

My ears were growing ever more sensitive to the noises of the jungle. When we first crashed on this mission just a few short days ago, I jumped at every sound. Every call of each small lizard in the forest made me raise my pistol, frantically searching the darkness for danger. The days of constant terror dulled my reaction but improved my perception. I noticed the change in the night's cacophony before we felt the ground begin to soften under our feet.

The trees were growing farther apart here, and they were smaller, heavier. With a sudden high-pitched squeal, Ms. Arnson sank into mud up to her knees. Brent and the General were closest to her and hauled her back onto the drier land where they were walking. Her cry sent a spike of panic through me as I started back into alertness.

"It's been getting wetter and wetter as we walk," she gasped, leaning on Brent. She pulled off her boots one by one and poured black water out of them onto the ground. "Let me see the map again."

Ms. Arnson didn't have a sat trans, so Brent called up the map of our approximate location on his. The bright glow blinded us for a moment in the darkness and we huddled together to block the glow from anything that might be looking our way.

Ms. Arnson pointed to the mottled patch of green and brown. "That's where we are now. This whole area. It's a swamp."

I vaguely recalled something about swamps from my Earth biology classes on board Horizon, but I couldn't think of anything specifically dangerous about them.

"What do we know about Ceti swamps?" the General asked her, and she shook her head.

"Not much. We've had a few teams do some scouting in the closest part to base, but we haven't had any reason to penetrate very deeply. I know what lived in Earth swamps. I have no idea what might live here."

I shivered in the cool night. Even Ms. Arnson doesn't know what's in there. Hardly reassuring.

"Maybe we can go around it, stay on more familiar ground," I ventured. The General looked back to the map, calculating the distance in his mind.

"It would take days. We'd have to cut back east and north almost all the way to the hills to avoid it."

"How did Shiro say Eden base was doing?" Brent asked. "How long do they think they have without this core?" He was still carrying the power core, the heaviest of all our packs. Shiro's name hung sodden in the air. I swallowed the lump it brought to my throat.

"They think they have about a week's worth of power in the two shuttle cores they're using. After that, the fences will go down. We don't know how long it will take the 'saurs to realize there's no juice anymore, but we can't count on very long. We have to be back to Eden base within a week." The General slapped a huge bloodsucker off his cheek. The light of the trans was attracting every insect in the jungle. The bloodsucker left a dark, wet stain on the General's face. It reminded me of ancient Earth history, primitive people painting their faces before a battle.

"Then we have to go through," Ms. Arnson said.

"I agree, sir. We can't take the time to go around." Brent nodded.

Nobody asked my opinion. I was almost too tired to have an opinion.

"But we have no idea what's in there," the General said, not disagreeing. Just a statement of fact.

"No, sir, we don't. But I don't see that we have any choice. Straight west is the fastest route back to Eden." Brent turned off his trans and a few of the bugs flew away, confused.

"Are we sure we can even get through?" I asked.

"No. And I think it would be stupid to attempt it in the dark. I just stepped right into a sinkhole I never even saw," Ms. Arnson said. "Luckily it wasn't very deep or I could have just disappeared under the water."

The General considered that. "Since we don't know what hunts in a swamp, and we don't know the terrain, there's no reason to assume travel at night is any safer than travel by day. Wolves probably won't hunt in a swamp." He paused and Ms. Arnson nodded. "Not sure about Gilas. And Rexes are out day and night, but we'll probably hear one coming even in the swamp." He came to a decision. "We'll sleep here on the ground for a few hours until sunup. Then we'll head into the swamp by day."

"General," I said. "There were Wolves."

"Where?" He raised his gun and spun around.

"Not here," I said. "Last night. Under the tree. I saw them go by."

He lowered his gun, peering into the trees. "Heading which way?"

I thought for a moment. My sense of direction was useless in this jungle. "I'm not sure. I think . . . the other way."

He shook his head. "Wolves. If they find us, we're done." He looked up at the tree canopy above our heads. "Everybody up."

Brent climbed behind me. "Nice going, Squirt. He was gonna

let us sleep on the ground for a couple hours."

"Feel free to stay down there if you want," I answered. "It's just Wolves."

He looked down at the soft, inviting ground, glared up at me, and followed me higher into the tree.

CHAPTER 15

I got the last watch of the night. Ms. Arnson woke me for the final hours before dawn and I sat up stiffly. My back protested. I felt like an old man. I used a little water from my canteen to rinse my face and felt several new welts where the bloodsuckers had feasted on the wounds from the Buzzer swarm while I slept. Scratching those bites kept me awake during my watch.

Dawn was hard to judge so deep in the forest, but as soon as I was able to see more than a few feet around me, I woke the others. We had no idea what waited for us in the swamp, but we knew what would hunt us on dry land once the sun heated the air and the daytime predators began to stir.

Ms. Arnson had us each cut a long branch off one of the trees.

"We'll poke them out ahead of us as we go to make sure we stay on solid ground." She demonstrated, pushing the stick out in front of her.

"Might keep us from stepping on something we don't see," agreed the General. Unlike most of Earth's venomous snakes, which wore bright colors to warn other animals of their deadly poison, Eden snakes were mostly brown and green. They would usually slither away if they heard a human approach, but you didn't want to startle one by stepping on it.

I kept looking over my shoulder as we started our day's trek, alert for the sway of brush, the glimpse of a gray scaled body that might be our only warning that the Wolves had found us. But we trudged on through the squelching mud, and I saw that Ms. Arnson was right. Wolves wouldn't be able to move quickly through this mire. They wouldn't have the element of surprise they relied on. There might be other dangers here, but Wolves weren't among them.

We had spent the past few days sleeping through the heat of the day in the treetops and traveling by night. Sweat poured off my forehead and stung my eyes in the humidity. I paused to cut a strip off the tail of my shirt, which I wrapped around my forehead to stop the drips. Brent was walking behind me, and he smiled.

"Good idea, Squirt."

I hated when the older guys called me that. My brother Josh had started it, and all his buddies adopted the nickname for me. When Josh was alive it had rankled me because it was silly. Now it just reminded me that he was gone.

Brent tied a sweatband around his own forehead and we followed the General and Ms. Arnson through the steamy swamp.

Brent still had both of his parents and two younger sisters back at base. His engineer dad was injured early in our tenure on this planet, paralyzed when a bullet fired by a soldier pierced his spine. If he'd realized what he'd done, the soldier who shot him would have felt terrible about it. But he'd been shooting at a solitary Wolf, probably a pack outcast, that had snuck up on the team working on the wind turbines. The soldier was torn apart before he could have realized he'd shot one of our few remaining engineers. If there had been more than that solitary Wolf, Brent would have lost his father that day.

Every now and then luck was with us, and Brent was one of the few who hadn't lost a family member to a bloody death. I stuck close to him, hoping his charmed good fortune would protect me, too.

We moved slowly, poking our walking sticks into the mud ahead of us. The swamp's mud dissolved into a maze of paths which Ms. Arnson called hummocks, dryer patches of ground with stagnant water all around. Froglike hoppers splashed into the dark pools as we approached. Occasionally we saw ripples farther out into the water as something larger paddled under the surface. Thick algae grew across the surface of the water, making it hard to distinguish our path.

We still walked beneath a canopy of trees, but here and there we could peek through to the deep blue of the sky. I smiled in spite of our perilous location. For the first ten years of my life, all I saw of sky was the black void, sparkling with distant stars, viewed through the thick glass of Horizon's portholes. Then we landed here and somehow that black sky turned blue when viewed from the ground. And pink in the sunrise, and orange in the sunset. During the day we couldn't see the stars at all, so bright was the sky. I still hadn't gotten over the strangeness of the daytime sky with its ever changing cycle of clouds and sunshine.

The 'saurs here in the swamp had never seen a human. Most of them were small, barely knee high. Some hung from the trees, others basked on downed logs over the water. They weren't afraid of us and didn't run, but all of them gave us a wide berth as we approached.

At noon we rested. There was nothing very solid to sit on and I felt my pants growing wet as I sat on the driest patch of ground I could find to eat my protein bar. We only had a few left for each of us. I didn't realize I was hungry until I started eating. Then my empty stomach woke up and grumbled its discontent. I made the bar last as long as I could, taking tiny bites to savor the bland taste. Ms. Arnson warned us not to fill our canteens from the puddles all around us.

"This is stagnant water. Who knows what kind of parasites live in this? Make your clean water last as long as you can." I wanted to guzzle it down in the stifling heat, but I sipped as she instructed.

"We can boil some tonight," Brent suggested.

"That's a last resort. We don't even know if boiling kills the stuff that lives here. But if we run out, then that's what we'll have to do," she agreed.

The General had been uncharacteristically quiet since we entered the swamp. I wondered if the deaths of our team members were haunting him. Five gone for sure. Then Shiro, though it hadn't been long since we left him. He might still be alive. Not for long.

The General sat down next to me now, squinting up into the bright day.

"How are you faring, Caleb?" he asked me.

"I'm fine, sir."

He sighed and looked down at his lap. "No, really, son. Are you holding up all right? I shouldn't have pushed your mother so hard to let you come . . ." he trailed off.

"It's okay, sir. You couldn't know," I shrugged. I just wanted to get moving again, but the General suddenly seemed to want to comfort me, though I had not given him any indication that I needed comfort.

"Your mom gave me an earful when I called in back in the hills."

"Yes, sir."

"Told me if I came back without you, she'd kill me herself. I believe her." He smiled.

"Yes, sir. I believe her, too." I smiled back, because I could tell he wanted me to.

"Whatever happens, stay close to me. We're not too far away. We're going to make it through this, son."

"Yes, sir."

He stood and offered me a hand up off the damp ground, clapping me on the shoulder with his other hand. I'd seen him use that gesture with Shiro and Brent. It made me feel less like a kid getting in his way and more like a soldier in his command.

"All right, team. Time to move out." We picked up our packs and weapons and our walking sticks and shuffled on through the steaming swamp.

CHAPTER 16

The General held up his fist, and we all halted without a word. He crouched down in the muck and we all followed suit, straining to see ahead.

Ms. Arnson was next in line, then me, then Brent in the rear. We all saw it at the same time.

I gasped as the vision of a 'saur the size of a Brachi unfolded out of the water in front of us. It had two giant humps on its long back, and a neck that let it stretch up to the distant treetops to browse. It chewed lazily, strings of swamp weeds hanging out of its mouth. Because its bottom half was submerged, I couldn't tell if it had legs or fins, or some kind of combination. It moved gracefully through the water for something so huge. Its green back matched the algae that covered the water's surface.

It paid us no attention at all and we cautiously stood up. The body of water it was wading in stretched away in front of us.

"Which way, sir?" Ms. Arnson whispered.

We crowded together to look at the map again.

"We're probably somewhere in here," the General said, pointing to an area of the swamp that looked the same as all the rest of it. The river curled away south of us. "If we head south, we risk running into the river delta where we probably can't cross." None of us wanted to have to swim, either in the opaque water of the swamp or the fast depths of the river. Swimmers didn't last long in Eden's waterways.

The General continued, squinting through the trees. "We head north and skirt this lake. Hopefully we won't have to go too far off our path."

The enormous 'saur didn't even mark our passing with a turn of its huge head, which reassured me. On dry land, even a Brachi gave us a glance to make sure of what we were. There were 'saurs our size that could take down a Brachi on land. But this creature wasn't worried about anything our size, and I felt my shoulders start to relax.

"I wish I had my equipment," Ms. Arnson fussed. We had left her piles of equipment on the crashed shuttle, taking only what we thought was most necessary.

"I can take a picture with my sat," I offered.

"Thanks! I'd love to study that thing. Maybe I can get back here soon," Ms. Arnson said.

I gaped at her. "Come back here? You want to come back out here? If we make it back to base, I'm never leaving the fence-line again," I said, realizing I sounded like a coward. But Ms. Arnson ignored that.

"I know what you mean. I'll be glad to sleep with an electric wire around me again, in a bed instead of a tree. But there's so much here we've never seen before. Most of the animals in here have never been described."

"Then you get to name them," I offered.

"I guess I do," she agreed. "I'm going to call the big one Nessie," she said with a laugh. I wasn't sure why that was funny, and it was an odd name for a 'saur.

"There must be whole families of Nessies out here. There's acres of swamp." She found that even funnier.

"Who would have thought? Families of Nessies." The General chuckled ahead of us.

"What's Nessie?" I asked.

Ms. Arnson smiled back at me. "There was a lake called Loch Ness on Earth in a country called Scotland. People believed there was a monster in it. A plesiosaur, maybe, left from when Earth had dinosaurs. They called it 'Nessie,' and it looked just like this one. Who knew it actually exists?"

The General muttered, "But not in Loch Ness anymore."

Ms. Arnson's smile faded at the sobering reminder. Earth was long gone. Scotland and Loch Ness hadn't existed for almost two hundred years.

As evening fell, the General reckoned we were about halfway through the swamp. We set up a makeshift camp on the highest hummock we could find.

"Do we risk a fire, sir?" Brent asked.

Fire scared the smaller 'saurs. But the heat sometimes attracted the larger ones. The General considered the request.

"We haven't seen anything around that posed us much danger. Let's try and find some dry wood."

"Maybe I can kill us something to eat," Brent suggested, and my stomach growled loudly at the thought of fresh meat.

The General agreed. "Good idea. You see what you can catch. Caleb, you and Sara try to find something dry to burn. Stay in sight." The darkness was falling quickly.

We gathered a few fallen logs that were mostly out of the water. There wasn't much to use as kindling since even the fallen leaves were squelched in the mud, but we got a few handfuls of brush and piled it up near the water's edge. I crouched with my back to the water and pulled out my firelighter.

The first few sparks hissed on the damp wood. I tried to light the driest bits, leaning down to blow gently on the tiny, sputtering flame.

The General crashed into me, a flying tackle that shoved me off my feet. I landed hard on my right elbow, with the General on top of me. He jumped to his feet and pulled me by the arm, slipping in the mud.

"What the . . ." I sputtered, dazed from the sudden hit. "What was that for?" I demanded.

The General had pulled his pistol and was aiming at something at the water's edge where I had just been crouching. I peeked around the stack of logs and saw the gaping mouth of a long, flat 'saur, half in and half out of the water. It had been lunging at me but got a mouthful of firewood instead when the General shoved me out of its path.

It closed its mouth and stared at us with dark, empty eyes. The General kept his weapon trained on the brown leathery head. Gunfire was dangerous. It could be heard for miles around, and the 'saurs who had learned about humans knew it was as good as a dinner bell. But not shooting could be just as dangerous.

The 'saur turned and slithered back into the water. A moment's ripple disturbed the green surface, then the water was flat and still, with no indication that sharp-toothed death lurked somewhere in the shallows.

CHAPTER 17

Brent dragged a dark scaled body behind him when he returned, his walking stick impaling the carcass.

"It just sat there. I walked up and speared it. What happened?" he asked, noticing our dilated eyes, our rapid breathing. My heart was still pounding from the nearness of my escape.

"We just found a new dinosaur," Ms. Arnson said, deceptively calm. "Stay away from the water's edge."

Brent looked quizzically at the bank where the saur's body had left a deep imprint in the mud. We pulled our firewood higher on the hammock and soon had a small blaze going. Ms. Arnson pulled out her sketchbook to make hasty drawings of the new 'saurs we had seen on this journey, including this small one that would be our dinner.

The General skinned Brent's kill and the smell of roasting meat made my mouth water. Ms. Arnson warned us to make sure it was cooked through, but we tore into the meat while it was still red in the middle, savoring the crisp edges. Juice dribbled down my chin and I wiped it with my fingers, licking them clean. We ate our fill and hung what remained from a tree branch to smoke overnight. It wouldn't dry by morning, but at least we'd have breakfast before we set out again.

I was far too keyed up to sleep, the adrenaline of my brush with death still zinging through my body. I took first watch and listened to Brent's quiet snoring, barely audible over the nighttime calls of the swamp. Every time something splashed into the water that surrounded us, I jumped, but nothing came lunging out of the night. Whether the 'saurs in the swamp were wary of our fire or just hadn't learned how delicious humans were, I didn't know or care.

I woke Ms. Arnson for her watch and stretched out on the boggy ground to sleep. I lay there for a few minutes, looking up at the glimpse of black sky visible through the holes in the treetops. One star shone brighter than the rest, because it wasn't a star at all. The light of Ceti's sun glinted off the dead husk of Horizon, drifting in its slowly decaying orbit overhead. Somewhere in its silent halls my father's body lay, along with all the others who didn't make it off the ship in the chaos after the explosion. In a few hundred years Horizon would probably come crashing down, burning in the atmosphere and falling in flaming ruin to the jungle below. I hoped it hit a lot of 'saurs when it fell.

★★★

We broke camp at dawn, chewing on the semi-dry strips of meat we'd hung out last night. I wanted fresh water, but not enough to get any nearer to the weed-choked edge than I had to. I sipped on the dregs that remained at the bottom of my canteen as I walked along.

"We should be out of this swamp and back onto dry land by late this afternoon," the General said. I still had no idea how he was reckoning our position. The swamp looked endless to me, and even with the sparser tree cover I still couldn't see enough stars to get any notion of our direction.

"I'll be glad to get out of this wet," Brent said. "My feet feel like they're getting moldy in my boots."

"But there's so much to see in here," Ms. Arnson said. Even surrounded by danger, she couldn't help getting excited about science. Most of the small 'saur faces that peeped quizzically at us from the branches and floating logs were new species no one had ever seen before. I knew she must be itching to photograph them, record them in her notebooks. She would have so much new information to teach the kids back at Eden.

I was mostly just glad to be finished with school. There weren't enough students in Eden to teach in classes, so we were all kind of crammed together in the same room. And there just hadn't seemed much point in continuing to teach us advanced math and physics when what Eden really needed was soldiers to keep it safe. Scholars like Ms. Arnson could keep all our scientific knowledge straight, but for me, shooting and tracking and staying alive was a lot more important. It wasn't like we were going to be flying anywhere anytime soon. We were down to our last few shuttles on the planet, and with no way to power our base, we had no hope of manufacturing anything that might help us get away from this place. When the last of the power ran out, when the metal ships rusted away to nothing and all the technology we brought from Earth decayed away, we'd be a primitive society. If any of us survived that long.

"Will we keep traveling in daylight once we leave the swamp, sir?" I asked.

"Negative. We'll stay on the edge until nightfall, then carry on from there."

So this was my last chance to walk in daylight until we made it back to base. Even though it was a lot more dangerous to travel by day, I hated skulking around in the dark. It made me feel like a shrew, skittering in the underbrush, jumping at every noise.

The tree cover began to darken as the ground began to firm

up under our feet. After a few yards, the General held up a fist and we all stopped behind him.

"That's as far as we go. Brent, you and Ms. Arnson find us a decent tree to get up until nightfall. Caleb, you come with me. We need to refill our canteens before we settle in."

Brent took the heavy pack with the power core off the General's shoulders and I collected everyone's canteens. Shiro's face popped into my mind, holding me fast when I panicked at the sleeping Gila. Of course I was going with the General. Because you don't trust me out of your sight for ten seconds.

"I can hear water moving up ahead. Should be a clear enough stream for us to risk getting close."

"Yes, sir," I answered, hoping he was right. I wasn't getting anywhere near a body of water I couldn't see into.

I tried to trail behind him, but he slowed his strides, and I had no choice but to fall in alongside him.

The General gave a low chuckle. "Your mom is worried to death. She didn't want me to take you on this mission. Seems she was right. As usual." He snorted softly.

"I'm old enough, sir. Josh was out on missions at my age." I regretted saying it as soon as the words came out of my mouth. The General had sent Josh on that last scouting mission. The one he never returned from.

"I know, son. And that's what I told her. Back on the ship, a boy your age would still be in school. Your biggest worry ought to be a math test or a literature essay. Instead you're out here in this scatting swamp. But there's just not much time for childhood on Ceti." The General didn't seem like he was talking to me anymore, but I was the only one around.

He continued, "I promised her I'd keep you safe out here, and I promised it again when I called in from the hills. She'll have my head when we get back."

He said it casually, like there was no chance we wouldn't return to base alive. But I knew better.

"She'll be so happy to see us, she won't kill you, sir," I said.

The General laughed. "I hope you're right. I'd love to see her happy. You remember back on Horizon before we got here? How she used to sing in that little group and we'd all come out to hear them? Your dad would stand there looking so proud of her. He was a good man, your dad."

"Yes, sir."

"Your mom and my Amalie were good friends on the ship. Things could have been so different . . ." he trailed off.

His wife Amalie had died within months of our landing in Eden. There were diseases here that humans had never been exposed to. Ms. Arnson said that was why we were so careful in our breeding, why we had brought so many frozen embryos with us. So our population wouldn't get inbred and some virus wipe us all out. But once all the Earth Children were born from those embryos, we should have enough people to keep our gene pool deep. That was the hope of the scientists who sent us out here two centuries ago. It seemed impossible now. Even if all the women survived the next few decades, we'd barely have enough population to keep us going. All that depended on us getting the power core back to buy us more time. Time to figure out some way to live here, some way to exist on this hostile world.

CHAPTER 18

"Things will get better when we get back to base with this core, son. It will buy us a little more time." The General took quiet steps on the damp ground.

"Time for what, sir?" I don't know why I asked.

"Time to scout farther, find someplace safer. Time to get our people moved somewhere we can plant our seeds, work the land. Somewhere we can be out in daylight to harvest crops without fear of death behind every tree. Somewhere we can really settle and raise our children knowing they have a good chance to live to grow up."

That was it, right there. The General had two grown daughters with Amalie. They were probably sitting with my mom back at base, worrying and wondering if we would ever return. His oldest daughter was pregnant, and I could see how that weighed on him. How could he be happy for his first grandchild when our lives here were so fragile? If we didn't get back to base soon, his daughter wasn't likely to live long enough to give birth at all. And the General wanted more than just this grandchild.

We lived in makeshift housing among our downed ships. Mom, Josh, and I shared rooms in the shuttle that brought us from Horizon, a secure place compared to the lean-tos and cobbled-up shacks a lot of other people had to make do with. When Josh didn't come back a few months ago, the General moved in with us.

And the General wanted a son. Mom had three kids in the proper order: the first with my dad, the second from the frozen straws of DNA from long-dead men on Earth, and the third our sweet Malia, an Earth Child from a frozen embryo placed aboard Horizon with some doomed couple's hope for immortality. So her next child, if she had one, could be another natural. The General was trying to convince her to give it a try, but Mom was too afraid, especially since Josh was gone. She held out little enough hope for our future here on Eden that she didn't want to bring another life into this awful place. I didn't blame her.

Radiation from Horizon's nuclear reactor meant that hardly anyone lived past fifty. The General was past forty already, and there wasn't much time left for Mom to have another baby, even if she'd wanted to.

The three years we'd been here had aged her, constant worry etching new lines around her eyes and mouth. She was still beautiful at thirty-seven, but the hopeful woman who had been in a singing group on Horizon, the happy Mom who looked at our dad with so much love—that Mom was gone.

I stumbled as the General stopped suddenly, pushing with his boot at something half buried in the wet dirt. "What's this?" he said.

We crouched down to look. Something small and metal protruded from the muck, mostly covered with the creeping ferns that grew everywhere in this swamp. The General cleared the ferns away with his knife, revealing more of the metal shine that had drawn his eye to the ground.

"What is it?" I asked. It was smaller than any of our satellites, and I didn't think any of the small drones had gotten launched from Horizon before the explosion.

"I'm not sure," the General said. There were markings in the metal, scratched lines that might have been etched there by the fall to Ceti. But the metal looked so shiny, brighter than any I'd seen. Everything on Horizon was over two hundred years old. This looked brand new. And the more I looked at the markings the more I became convinced it was some kind of writing, unlike any I recognized.

"Can we carry it back?" I asked. I looked around, suddenly struck by the unsettling notion that the 'saurs might not be the only life on this planet. Who had made this object, and when? It was buried deeply enough in the foliage that it must have been there for years, long before Horizon entered Eden's atmosphere. We had never found the slightest indication that any other intelligent species had lived here. The hairs on the back of my neck raised and I squinted into the vegetation, searching for some unseen observer. I saw nothing but empty swamp.

The General tapped it with the flat of his knife. It made a soft ping. "Whatever it is, it's been here quite a while."

My fingers traced the markings on the object's face. "These lines look . . . intentional. Like some kind of letters."

"It's no language I've ever seen."

We dug at the sides of the metal object trying to free it.

"I don't think we're going to get it loose easy enough." The General glanced up at the darkening sky. "And I don't think this came from Horizon. I'm not sure where it came from. But it will have to stay here a while longer. Let's get these canteens filled and get back to the others."

I hurried to catch up with the General, glancing back over my shoulder at the strange object.

There was no warning rustle, no telltale shape. They sit so

still, blending into the bushes around them. If I'd been walking on the left side, it would have been me. But I wasn't, and when the Gila stood up out of the brush and whipped its tail around faster than we could think, the General took the sting.

It hit him in the thigh, tearing open a great gash in his pants. He fell into me and I caught him, lowering him down to the damp ground. The Gila crouched back in the bushes, content to wait for its poison to work. Four-legged and built low to the ground, they weren't fast movers, except that tail. They didn't need to be. When their venom coursed through a body, they could stroll along behind at their leisure until their victim collapsed, gasping for air. The doctors said their venom was some kind of neurotoxin that paralyzed the muscles, including the diaphragm. The General had about twenty seconds left to breathe.

I grabbed frantically at his shoulders, trying to drag him away from the crouching Gila but he reached up and held my arm, stilling me.

"Go while you can!" he gasped.

"I won't leave you, sir," I whispered, clutching his arm, though we both knew it was futile. Hardly anyone survived Gila venom, even if they had a team of doctors and all of Eden's medical supplies right there. Out here, he had no chance at all.

"Don't let it get you, too. Get back to the team, get back to Eden. It's all on you. Tell your mother . . ."

The General's throat seized up before he could finish the sentence. His eyes bulged wide in panic as he twitched helplessly on the ground, unable to move, unable to breathe.

I backed away from the grisly scene and raised my pistol. At least I could kill the Gila that got the General. I sighted the beast's neck, the only place soft enough for a bullet to penetrate. But before I could pull the trigger, the General's voice echoed in my ear, a memory of my training that I hoped never to use.

"If a team member is truly lost, don't waste a shot. You'll only accomplish two things: alerting every other 'saur in the vicinity to your location, and possibly just enraging the 'saur you meant to kill. If your man is lost, let the 'saur have its meal and use the time to get the rest of your team to safety."

He had told us that near the beginning of training, when we'd first landed and started to figure out the dangers that threatened us here. I felt like decades had passed since then.

The Gila slowly emerged from the bushes, paying me no special mind. I backed up farther, unable to look away as it lowered its broad, green-scaled head to sniff at the General's still body. Its wide nostrils flared, a strand of drool dripping from its fetid maw.

"I'm so sorry, General Carthage," I whispered, as the Gila opened its mouth to feed. I turned and ran into the swamp.

CHAPTER 19

I ran as fast as I could, partly to warn Ms. Arnson and Brent, and partly to escape the horrible sound of the 'saur chewing.

"The General . . . the General," I panted, skidding to a stop when I found them.

"Where is he? What happened?" Brent took a step in the direction I had just come from. I grabbed his arm.

"Don't go. A Gila . . . it got the General. It's too late."

Brent's muscles softened under my hand as he sagged down. I let go of his arm and he buried his hands in his hair, pushing his palms into his eyes.

Ms. Arnson looked down at her boots. None of us knew what to say.

"Fly free, General Carthage," I said quietly.

"Fly free, General," they echoed.

The three of us stood there in the swampy forest, listening to the sounds of the evening jungle.

Brent pulled himself together first.

"All right, team. I'm the highest rank left, so I guess it's up to me," Brent said. He certainly had a lot more experience than I did, and Ms. Arnson wasn't even in the army. I doubted she even knew how to shoot the gun she was carrying.

"Let's get up the tree until it's dark. We need to rest and figure out what we're going to do."

Ms. Arnson and I agreed and we started to climb. Brent carried the reactor core pack and Ms. Arnson and I divided up the remaining food. We only had the two canteens I'd been carrying; the General had been carrying the other two. The Gila wouldn't eat them, and we might be lucky enough that it wouldn't carry the General's remains away with it. We might get the other two canteens back, but that would mean searching whatever was left of the General to retrieve them. I didn't think it was worth it. We settled high in the branches, startling a number of the small climbing 'saurs that were browsing among the leaves.

Brent spoke in a quiet voice. "So what do we have?"

"Sir?" I replied, not sure what he meant. Brent had never been "sir" before, but he was the leader of this pathetic mission now.

"How much food, how much water? I have the core," he said, setting the reactor core in the V of the branch he was sitting on. "Do we have rope? Ammo?"

We searched the bags. There were three protein bars left, enough rope to tie us all safely for the night, plenty of rounds for our weapons and precious little water. The sun was beginning its descent. We had a few hours until nightfall.

"All right, then. Let's tie in for the rest of the evening. We'll set out again at full dark. The General said we were about two nights out. So we travel through tonight, and hope to reach Eden tomorrow night."

He sounded so optimistic. Like he really thought we'd make it. I pictured the General and wondered if Brent was trying to fool us, or himself.

Ms. Arnson took first watch, but I didn't sleep at all. My watch passed without incident, and I nodded off for a few minutes during Brent's.

I awoke to cooler air and darkness.

Brent consulted the map on his sat trans, and I did the same.

"We must be somewhere here," he said, pointing to the line of darker green which we now knew marked the edge of the swamp. "If we head due west, we should get there eventually."

Ms. Arnson looked over my shoulder at my map. "Maybe we should head northwest, try to get up into the hills there." She pointed to a brown area of dead rock, a point in the foothills of the empty mountains that we had taken refuge in the night Jack died.

"We could talk to Eden from there, let them know we're coming," I agreed.

Brent shook his head. "There's nothing up there but rock, no food. No reason to go out of our way. Eden will know when we get there. Calling them a day out won't help them or us."

"So, which way then?" I asked him.

He pointed out through the treetops. "The sun set right over there, so that's due east. We go that way." He pointed in the opposite direction.

We climbed down out of the branches and our shoes squelched in the mud at the bottom.

"Should we try to find the other canteens?" I asked, dreading the answer.

"No. We have two. That will have to do us for two days."

I sighed, relieved not to have to search the site where the General had died. I thought about mentioning the strange metal object the General had found that had distracted us from the vigilance this planet required. But I didn't think Brent would be interested.

We set off toward the west. We risked turning on our

flashlights to search the edge of a wide stream before we crossed it. There weren't any Gators, as Ms. Arnson had named them, but some large fish darted out of the beams as our lights played into the deeper pools. Each of us drank a canteen full of fresh water, then we refilled them before splashing across. The water was cold and seeped straight into my boots. I would have strangled a Wolf for dry socks.

Two hours into the night we felt the first tremor. We froze, listening. The jungle had gone silent at the Rex's approach, a bad sign that it was heading in our direction. A lot of the larger 'saurs shook the ground when they walked, but nothing matched the pounding footfalls of a T-rex. That concussion had saved countless lives over our three years here, giving men time to dive for cover before the Rex approached.

The ground vibrated again, closer. Again. We turned our heads, trying to pinpoint the direction it was coming from. We didn't dare turn on a light and reveal our position but my hand kept straying to the flashlight on my belt. The darkness was pressing in on me as the vibrations trembled through my feet.

I looked up at the trees around us, hoping to see one with good low branches for a frantic climb out of reach but none looked inviting.

We didn't know which way to move, but then Ms. Arnson grabbed my arm and started to pull me. I followed as quietly as I could. We crowded into a hollow at the base of a huge tree, pressing our backs up against the damp wood. Brent was the last one in, blocking the opening with his body. We held our breath as the Rex's steps pounded through the jungle.

Hardly any of the forest's glow penetrated past Brent's shoulders, but there was no mistaking the darkness when the Rex's shadow loomed over our tree.

A huge clawed foot landed inches from where we huddled, not breathing, not moving. Brent could have reached out and stroked the talon, longer than his arm and sharper than his knife. The Rex's skin was mottled yellow. Two small scars marred the skin of its toe, the result of some small creature's futile attempt to free itself from the Rex's attack.

A terrible roar split the night, driving my eardrums straight into my skull. I clapped my hands over my ears to muffle the blast, making a strangled sound inaudible over the Rex's call. An answering roar echoed from somewhere far to the south.

The Rex turned away from us, its huge tail striking the side of the tree where we were hiding. I felt the impact of the blow and covered my head with my arms as dirt from the rotted tree stump rained down around us.

The tremors faded as the Rex moved off into the jungle and we all sighed. After a few minutes of silence, the noise of the jungle started up again and we crawled out from the hollow on shaky legs. I stumbled into the Rex's enormous footprint. We crept away into the darkness.

CHAPTER 20

"We're lost."

All three of us knew it, but Ms. Arnson said it. We had been relying on the General's sense of direction to carry us safely back to Eden base. Now the General was gone.

Once the sun fully set, we had only the forest's natural phosphorescence to guide our trail and no indication of which way to go. We tried to continue in as straight a line as we could, but the thick tree canopy hid the stars from our view and I suspected we were veering off course. I hoped we could find a clearing to make contact with the satellites, but then I thought of Shiro, whose one careless step likely cost him his life while trying to crawl out to open sky.

The forest's glow was starting to dim as the chemicals on the leaves were used up over the course of the night. We were only a couple of hours from dawn and the fresh dangers of daylight.

We stopped walking and took turns drinking from our two remaining canteens. The protein bars were gone and we chewed on the last of the dried strips of meat from the 'saur Brent had killed in the swamp.

"We need to contact the satellites, get our bearings. Eden is tiny and we could walk right past it if we're off even a little bit." Brent tapped his sat trans, willing the little screen to connect with a satellite it couldn't see.

"I'm the lightest," I said. "I could try to get high enough in one of these trees to get through."

Brent peered up into the darkness, but Ms. Arnson answered.

"You'll never get high enough. The canopy is too thick and the branches at that height won't hold even your weight. If you tried, you'd fall."

I shuffled my foot in the dirt, digging a trench with the toe of my boot. "Well, we have to do something. Eden doesn't have long without this core." I tapped the pack I carried. The core was heavy, so we each took our turns.

Brent stood silent, thinking. He wasn't a natural leader, not like the General or Shiro. Not like my brother Josh had been. But he was all we had left.

"We need to get somewhere we can get through." He called up the map on his trans, glowing in the pre-dawn darkness. "We have to be somewhere around here," he pointed to an area in the green all around. "If we go north a bit we should come to the spur of the hillside here." He pointed again, to a barren brown spike where the rocky mountainous cliffs angled down near our presumed location.

"It's kilometers out of our way," I protested. "The General said we didn't have time."

"I know. But we can't risk missing Eden because we can't navigate from here," Brent said. "We'll head up that way and send a signal, figure out how long we have. Then we'll make a beeline for Eden once we're sure of our course."

Ms. Arnson looked around at the dark jungle. "So which way is north?"

The sun hadn't yet started to brighten the sky. We didn't know.

"Not sure," Brent sighed. He straightened his shoulders, coming to a decision.

"Let's rest here until dawn. Once we see where the sun rises we'll know where to go. We can travel by day once we're sure. It can't be more than a few hours to the base of the hills. It will be clear enough there to contact base."

"Are you sure?" I asked. "The General didn't want us traveling by day. Too dangerous." I looked to Ms. Arnson for support.

"I agree, but I'm not sure we have much choice." She shook her head. "Traveling by night hasn't been all that safe anyway."

I didn't like it. Ms. Arnson was right; we'd lost over half our party by following the General's plan. But I doubted we'd have gotten this far without his leadership. The night had its dangers, but the day was deadly.

We sat on a fallen log, resting our tired feet. I pulled my boots off one by one and emptied out the dirt and leaves that seemed to accumulate inside them no matter how tightly they were tied. My aching back popped as I stretched and tried to ignore the feeling that we were making a huge mistake. I tried one more time to convince Brent.

"Eden base sits on the east bank of the river. I think if we just keep moving west by night, we'll eventually hit the river even if we miss the base. Then we could just follow the bank until we get there."

"Follow it which way, though?" he asked. "If we miss Eden and run into the river, how will we know if we're north or south of base? We might turn the wrong way and end up hours away in the wrong direction."

I didn't think we'd end up that far off, not if we just kept going the same way the General had been leading us. But I didn't say anything else. Brent had rank. Brent was our leader now. Right or wrong, I would follow.

My eyelids felt heavy and my head kept nodding forward. It had been too long since we'd slept well, too long since we'd eaten. We were worn down, exhausted from fear and loss. I must have dozed off because the next time I opened my eyes there was sunlight angling through the treetops.

"Brent, Ms. Arnson," I whispered. "Wake up. It's daylight."

I looked around the forest. It looked so different in the light. I had gotten used to walking in the dim glow of the nighttime leaves. Now their vibrant green hurt my eyes. The morning was alive with sound, the less-familiar calls of the small 'saurs who hunted the treetops in the day. Soon the larger 'saurs would stir as the ground warmed beneath them. It was time to move.

CHAPTER 21

We moved faster in daylight. It gave us a false sense of security to be able to look out through the trees and think we were seeing all that was there, even if we knew most of the 'saurs were camouflaged in some way. Even those that had brightly colored crests or flashy red scales could blend in with the huge flowers that opened by day to catch the light that filtered through the canopy.

I scanned the path ahead, analyzing every shape. Even so, I didn't see the herd of browsing 'saurs until we were almost on top of them.

"Watch out," Ms. Arnson whispered, grabbing at the back of Brent's shirt.

There were at least twenty of them, spread out through the trees, nibbling on the damp fronds and scraping bark off the tree trunks with their bottom teeth. No knife-sharp claws or wicked fangs on these, but they had stocky bodies encased in thick armor to protect them from all but the strongest predator's bites. The young ones capered around, playing some kind of lumbering game while the adults shook fruits from the treetops. The young ones trotted over to the fallen fruit to share in the sweet meal.

"Can we eat that kind of fruit?" I asked Ms. Arnson. My stomach growled at the thought.

"Not sure. We can eat most of the tree fruits that grow here, but not many of the berries." I knew that from my survival training. Never eat the green berries, only the red ones. Someone had died learning that lesson.

"Think we can get some of it?" I asked, hopeful.

We all crouched down.

"You're the fastest," Brent said to me. "Think you can run over there and grab some without getting trampled?"

I considered it. I knew not to get any closer to a 'saur than I had to, not even a plant-eater. The General would never have let me go. But hunger made me reckless.

"I think I can."

I stood up and crept toward the feasting 'saurs. They had already eaten most of what they pulled down from the trees. One of the adults saw me and trumpeted an alarm. They all raised their heads to stare at me.

I lunged toward them and scooped up a few fruits off the ground. A lot of them had been trampled and mushed into the dirt, but I got several and tucked them into my shirt. I turned to run back to Ms. Arnson and Brent. The herd panicked at my quick movement and suddenly the ground was shaking as they all tried to scatter at once.

I dodged to the right, narrowly avoiding a collision with a small one heading straight for me. It didn't even see me, plunging right through where I was just standing. I ran as fast as I could, jumping over logs and careening through dense brush. Finally I stopped near where I had left Brent and Ms. Arnson. I turned back to see the last of the herd disappearing into the trees.

"Nice job. What did you get?" Brent asked.

I opened my shirt. Six large orange fruits, mostly intact.

"What do you think?" Brent asked Ms. Arnson.

She picked one of the fruits out of my hands. Pulling her knife from her belt she cut the fruit neatly in half. It smelled ripe and fresh and my mouth watered.

She sniffed it carefully, then rubbed the cut surface over her lips.

"I think these are okay, but let's wait a few minutes. If they're poisonous, I should feel some tingling on my lips."

"Let's keep moving, then," I suggested. We each took two of the orange fruits and continued our walk.

After a few agonizing minutes I ran out of patience.

"Well, are your lips burning? Can we eat them?"

Ms. Arnson smiled back at me. She was walking between Brent and me, the leader and the rear guard.

"I think we're okay."

She didn't even finish the sentence before I had my knife out. I cut big chunks off the fruit and stuffed them in my mouth. Sticky juice ran down my chin and I wiped it on my filthy sleeve, grinning. It tasted sweet and fresh. It was the finest fruit I ever ate.

"Oh, it's so good," Brent murmured up ahead and I laughed. An empty stomach made the poorest meal into a feast.

A full stomach improved my mood. I was still exhausted, but the sun was brightening my outlook along with the rest of the forest. Scuttling around in the dark was for shrews. Humans were meant to walk by day.

Ms. Arnson and Brent fell into quiet conversation ahead of me.

"How long until we reach the hills?" she asked.

"Hopefully no more than another hour. We should be close."

"I hope Eden is okay." She said this quietly, almost to herself, but Brent answered.

"They'll be all right. We'll get the core back in time." He

sounded confident.

Ms. Arnson didn't answer for a while. Then she said, "You have both your parents at base, right? And two little sisters?"

"Yeah. We were really lucky. We were all together when Horizon went bust and we all got on a shuttle together."

Ms. Arnson turned to me. "And you have your mom and your little sister?" She didn't mention Josh. Everyone knew about Josh.

"Mom and Malia, yeah," I answered. "What about you?"

"Just me," she said quietly. "My parents didn't make it onto the shuttle with me, and neither did my sister. Maybe they got on one of the others. I like to think they're still alive out there somewhere. Like maybe they landed somewhere safer, some other part of this dino-scat planet where they could survive." She said it with surprising heat. It was the first time I had heard Ms. Arnson speak of Ceti with anything other than awe. A new planet with life completely unknown to humans, Ceti should have been a naturalist's dream. But even Ms. Arnson's reverence for the life here had its limits. I wanted to comfort her, to pat her on the shoulder or something, but even though my schooling was done and we were just three people lost in a jungle, she was still my former teacher.

"Maybe the other shuttles are on another continent, wondering why they can't contact us," I suggested.

Ms. Arnson smiled. "Maybe there aren't any dinosaurs there, and they're all sitting around getting fat on fruit."

Brent chimed in. "I bet they're sitting out in the sun, fishing by a river that's not full of monsters. I bet they're . . ." He stopped abruptly and held up a fist like the General calling a halt.

We all stood still, listening, looking over our shoulders.

The hairs on the back of my neck stood up when I heard the click. It came from behind us. It was answered by another click off to our left. And then another, to our right. My hand shook as I reached for my pistol. A Wolf pack had found our trail. We were surrounded.

CHAPTER 22

We crouched down with our backs together, each facing a different direction.

"What do we do?" Ms. Arnson hissed.

Brent and I spoke at the same time.

"Shoot at the neck," he said.

"Get up a tree right now," I said.

We each realized what the other one had just said.

"We don't have time to get up a tree," he whispered. "They're close. You need two hands to climb, we'd have to put the guns away."

"We don't know how close they are. And we don't know how many. If there's more than three, we're dead even if we all hit one on the first shot. They'll be on us before we get a second one," I argued.

The clicking sounded again, closer. Still only three clicks, but that didn't mean anything. Wolves were coordinated. They listened to their leaders, unlike humans.

I didn't wait to hear what Brent said next. I holstered my pistol and took Ms. Arnson's arm. We ran for the nearest tree. Brent knew he couldn't take a Wolf pack alone; he had no choice but to follow us.

Ms. Arnson was carrying the power core and it weighed her down. I swung up into the lowest branch I could find and reached down to pull her up. She was struggling to get a leg over the branch.

"Drop the pack!" I told her, and she did. It made a soft sound when it landed in the soil. Lighter without it, Ms. Arnson made it up onto the branch. I climbed higher to make room and Ms. Arnson followed me up.

Brent jumped up behind us, grabbing the branch. And out of the brush, the Wolves appeared.

A streak of gray shot past me under the tree and Brent screamed. His panicked face looked up at mine and I scrambled down to try to reach him.

The lead Wolf hung from his leg, shaking its head. The 'saur stood on its hind legs, and the front ones pawed the air as it tried to pull Brent off the branch.

"Help me!" he yelled and I crashed past Ms. Arnson in the tree. She was screaming, too, scrambling up higher.

I reached Brent and locked my hands under his shoulders. I pulled with all my strength.

The Wolf was stronger. It whipped its head from side to side, tearing at the flesh of Brent's leg. He lost his grip on the branch and started to slide away from me. I gripped him as hard as I could, but his arms slipped through my hands. I made one final lunge to grab his wrist, but only managed to graze his skin with my fingertips as he made a gargling cry and fell to the ground.

I lost my balance and pitched forward. Two more Wolves

lunged at the trunk of the tree just beneath me. My shirt tightened as Ms. Arnson grabbed at my collar from above, preventing my fall to the snapping jaws below. I hooked my arm around the branch and we climbed for our lives.

At the base of the tree, four more Wolves had appeared. There were seven in the pack, and I turned my head away from the horrific sounds beneath me.

Ms. Arnson and I climbed and climbed, and when the trunk began to narrow and the branches got dangerously thin we stopped, panting.

She looked at me with wild eyes.

I grabbed her shoulder and held her still. "It's okay, we're okay. They can't climb." She had taught us about Wolves. Now I was telling her. "They can't get us up here. We're safe up here," I kept repeating it over and over. "We're safe."

Finally her eyes cleared and her hands stopped shaking so hard. She swallowed and looked down.

"Don't," I warned her. "Don't look down. He's gone. There's nothing we can do. It's just you and me now."

She wrapped her arms around the tree and closed her eyes.

"You were right," she whispered. "You said it was too dangerous by day. The General knew it, and you were right."

"The General was always right," I agreed. I took deep breaths, trying to steady myself.

"And you were right about the Wolf pack. There were too many. If we'd stayed down there and tried to shoot, we'd all be dead."

It was true. Instinctively I had known that our only chance was to flee. Brent had hesitated, and it had cost him his life.

I had one of the canteens around my neck, and I took a long drink, then handed it to Ms. Arnson. It seemed to calm her.

"So what do we do now? We can't get down?"

It took me a second to realize she was talking to me. She was asking me what to do. Because I was the only soldier left.

Oh, scat. It's up to me.

I thought for a few minutes.

"They'll eat, and then hopefully they'll move off. We'll wait until well into the night when they'll be too cold to chase even if they're close by. Then we'll come down and move on."

"But I dropped the power core." Her eyes were filling up with tears.

"It's okay. It's not food, so they won't eat it. We'll find it when we go down and we'll just keep going. It's all we can do. Just keep going."

"Okay." She turned away from me, and I could tell she was crying. I wasn't sure what to say, so I just kept quiet.

Hours passed. We tied ourselves to the tree with the rope from my pack and took turns trying to sleep. The Wolf pack clicked and fussed at the base of the tree far below, looking up into the branches where we waited. Eventually they gave up and moved off into the jungle, clicking in what sounded to me like a satisfied way.

You got Brent. You got Jack and Shiro and the General. But you won't get Ms. Arnson. And you won't get me.

CHAPTER 23

We stayed in the tree for a few more hours. I wanted to be sure the Wolves were far enough away and torpid enough in the cool air for us to get some distance between us and them. They were scent trackers, and they were faster than humans. We needed to move quickly.

The Wolves left nothing of Brent behind, for which I was grateful. I hadn't wanted Ms. Arnson to have to see the remains of someone she knew. She wasn't a soldier. It would have upset her.

It took us a few minutes of searching to find the power core. The Wolves had torn holes in the bag since it smelled like us, but as I hoped, they had no use for the heavy, solid metal core. We put it into our one remaining pack and I hoisted it on to my shoulders. I would carry it the rest of the way.

Ms. Arnson carried what remained of our supplies: some rope, our ammo, and the canteen. I had two pistols and Ms. Arnson had one.

"Do you know how to shoot?" I asked her.

"I know how. I'm not great, but I can hit a stationary target."

I didn't answer that any targets we had to shoot at out here were not likely to be stationary. She knew it.

"Well, let's just hope it doesn't come down to shooting."

I had watched where the sun set and we headed off to the west. Maybe Brent had been right, that we should be heading north toward the open hills to make contact, but so many days had passed since we spoke to Eden base. I felt the pressure of those days. Did they still have power? Were they still alive? Hours could make the difference, and I didn't want to waste any time.

We talked quietly as we walked, alert for danger. The peaceful noises of the jungle reassured us, and although the pack felt heavy on my back, I didn't complain.

A shallow, fast-moving stream rippled through the jungle and we waded in. The water was cool from its mountainous origin, but this time I didn't mind it soaking through my socks. If the Wolf pack woke up tomorrow morning and decided to follow our scent trail, they should lose us right here. Ms. Arnson wasn't happy about filling our canteens again, but we had no choice. At Eden base we had water purification chemicals. Out here we had nothing. But we'd die of dehydration before any water-borne parasite could kill us. We continued walking in the stream bed, stumbling over rocks in the dim light. It was leading us farther north than I had intended, but the danger of the pack tracking us made it worth the extra time.

"Poor Malia," Ms. Arnson said.

"What do you mean?"

"This is the second dad she's lost in her six years."

"The General wasn't her dad," I replied, out of habit. But that vehemence was softening in his absence. Our dad, Horizon's captain, dead this three years, wasn't actually her father, either, nor mine. But the General had loved Malia just like he had loved our mom. He'd been a father figure to my little sister since we landed here. And to me, I supposed, though I hadn't wanted a father figure.

"No, but she thought of him as her dad."

"How do you know?" I asked.

"I'm her teacher, just like I was yours on the ship."

I thought about that as we walked. Malia had been so little when our father died. She probably didn't remember what he looked like. The only father she had really known was the General. As much as I'd pushed him away, she had needed him. She'd still need him. Our real father had died to ensure we all got safely off Horizon. And now the General had died trying to ensure that my father's death wasn't in vain. We had to survive. And if I made it back, I had to make sure Malia knew that the General had died for her. For all of us.

"Malia's going to be crushed," I said.

Ms. Arnson nodded. "She'll need her big brother. She's just as bright as you and Josh."

The mention of my brother's name still brought a stabbing pain to my chest, and a memory came through, as vivid as the moment I experienced it.

I sat across the table from Josh as we breakfasted on honey and fruit.

"So what's your mission this time?" I asked him, licking my sticky fingers.

"Scouting and hunting, just like always."

I always wanted to hear all about his missions. My training was almost complete and soon I'd be heading out on my own, maybe on the same team as my brother. I couldn't wait. I lived for his stories of the adventure outside the fence.

"Bring back a T-rex this time," I teased him.

"No problem. What else would you like?"

I thought for a moment. "Three Brachis. Maybe one of those smaller 'saurs with the big frill on the neck. And a snake as big as the shuttle."

He pretended to consider my request.

"We'll have to bring the Brachis back in pieces."

"Yeah, they're too big to fit through the gate," I laughed.

"But the snake we can just drag right through long ways," he said.

My mom broke in. "If you see a snake out there that's as big as our shuttle, don't get anywhere near it. It would swallow you whole." She smiled like she was joking along with us, but she was also being serious. She worried the whole time Josh was out, no matter how many armed men he was with. I worried, too. Too many men hadn't come back.

After we finished eating, Josh hugged Mom and Malia and tousled my hair, which he knew I hated. It was such a little kid gesture, and I was almost a full soldier. But I let it slide, like I always did when he was heading out on a mission.

He said the same thing he always said to me when he left. "Take care of them."

And I answered the same as I always did. "I will."

He headed off toward the gate where his patrol was gearing up. I went the other way to my training class. The General was training all of us who were even close to old enough to go out. There were fourteen boys in my class. I was the oldest and the closest to graduating. In a few short months I would be joining Josh at the gate, boarding a tank or a shuttle or gearing up for a night mission on foot.

I looked over my shoulder and saw his back as he disappeared around the side of the downed transport that marked the edge of the fence-line.

His mission should have been back in five days. They had been with Commander Richards, one of the General's top men. He should have been able to keep them safe. They were only supposed to go two days' ride out, scouting for anything that might help us survive here and to bring back meat. They never called in, and they never returned.

So I did what Josh asked me to do. I took care of Mom and Malia as best I could.

The heavy power core on my back was digging into my hipbone, but Eden needed it to survive. Mom and Malia needed it. I hitched the strap up higher on my shoulder and walked on through the darkness.

CHAPTER 24

Ms. Arnson and I walked on. The stream curved as it flowed down from the distant hills, and I concentrated on our direction.

When the first rays of sun illuminated the highest branches of the canopy, I knew we had gone off course. We were heading northwest, not due west as I had planned. We had lost valuable time and were no closer to Eden.

"We need to head more that way," I said, pointing in what I hoped was the correct direction. If we had walked straight, we would have been there by now. I didn't know how far away we were, but I knew if we kept moving west, we'd hit the deep wide river that flowed past our base. We were certainly too far north by now, so if we turned south when we hit the river's bank, we'd run right into Eden.

"Shouldn't we be looking for a tree soon? It's getting awfully light." Ms. Arnson's shoulders sagged and her head was low. We needed to find Eden today. With no food and not enough water, we were running out of energy as surely as our home base was.

"Let's push on a little way. We must be pretty close by now." I strained my ears, hoping to hear the rush of flowing water, but the sounds of the forest drowned out any hope of that.

We walked on, sweating out fluid we couldn't afford to lose. We shared the last of the water in the canteen. Ms. Arnson looked at me as she passed it to me for the final drops. She said nothing, but her sunken eyes told the story. She was losing hope.

"We just need to get to the river," I told her, putting as much enthusiasm into my voice as I could muster, which wasn't much. "Then we'll follow it right down to base. They can hook up the core and it will all be okay."

She nodded, eyes lowered.

It felt strange to be talking to her like this. She had been my teacher, too. But now it seemed our roles had reversed. She knew more about the plants and animals here than I did, but I was the soldier. Our survival was up to my training, and that thought made me smile a little. I turned away from her. I didn't want her to think I was not taking this seriously. But I had to admit, I liked being talked to like an adult. Like a soldier. Like someone who had something to offer. I couldn't let anything happen to Ms. Arnson or the power core. Eden was depending on me. I straightened up under the weight of the heavy pack.

"It will be all right, Sara," I said.

A tiny smile quirked her lips.

"Lead on, soldier," she replied.

★★★

The jungle was brightening. Sunlight streamed into a small clearing ahead. I stopped at the forest's edge, peering out through the thick tree cover. A great hulking shape sat silent in the middle of the grassy field. It was already starting to overgrow with vines, but the rusty metal showed through the planet's attempt to swallow it up. A tank.

It ran on thick treads that chewed up the underbrush and clawed through the trees. Eight men and their supplies fit inside and a large top-mounted weapon fired a missile powerful enough to take down a Rex in full charge. This one couldn't have been here too long. We brought two down from Horizon on the last transports. One sat in Eden base—

I froze. The other was last seen growling away through the gates, heading off on a scouting mission. Josh's mission. My brother Josh had left Eden aboard this tank.

Why had they abandoned it here? What had made them leave its safety, venturing out into the forest to their deaths? It stood in a large enough clearing that its communications equipment would have been able to reach the satellites. If anyone had survived and hidden in the tank, they could have called in to base. No call had come, no word from Josh and his team of soldiers who ventured out that morning three months ago.

"Let's get to the tank. Even if it doesn't have power, we can still get a trans signal from there. We'll see where we are and let Eden know we're coming."

Sara agreed with my plan.

I stepped out into the bright sunlight and a mist of tiny insects swarmed my sweaty face. Batting them away I took cautious steps through the grass. Clearings like this were dangerous. We couldn't see predators hiding in the trees, but they could see us out in the open. Crossing the field in daylight was risky, but I couldn't take my eyes off the tank, the last connection I had to my brother.

Halfway across the field I heard the sound.

Click.

Behind us in the trees.

Click, click.

To our left.

Click.

To our right.

I didn't know if it was the same Wolf pack that had killed Brent. If they had tracked us through the morning, loping along with their heads low to the ground, sniffing out the hated scent of the prey that had evaded them the day before. Or if this was a different pack, lucking in to an easy kill, stupid food walking through a bright clearing in plain view. It didn't matter.

"Run!" I screamed, and took off toward the tank.

The power core bounced painfully into my kidneys with each stride. Sweat and bugs ran into my eyes, half blinding me in the hot sun. I couldn't hear if Sara was behind me or next to me. I couldn't hear the clicking of the pack. But I knew they would be on us in seconds. I pounded through the thick grass toward the tank's overgrown side.

I reached it and climbed as fast as I could, feet slipping on the huge treads. I gripped the vines and hauled myself up, reaching for the lowest rung of the metal ladder built into the huge hull. Grunting with the effort, I pulled myself up onto the tread and turned around.

Sara was right behind me. And the Wolves were right behind her.

Four of them were converging on her from behind and to the sides. She wasn't going to make it. She didn't look up as she ran, couldn't see them coming.

I dropped the heavy power core off my shoulders and drew my pistols.

Steady. I crouched down on the tread, steadying my arm on my knee. My heart was pounding so hard I could see my pulse in the sight of my pistol, a tiny waver in my aim with each beat. My sweaty hands trembled on the grip. Squeeze the trigger, don't pull. The General's firearm training echoed in my head. I squeezed.

The crack of the report echoed across the clearing. The Wolf I had aimed at, the one that was closest to Sara, stumbled and flipped over, skidding across the wet grass. It immediately stood up again on three legs, limping toward its prey. I couldn't see the wound my bullet made in its tough hide, but I had obviously hit it in one of its thick front legs. I aimed at the next closest beast.

Crack.

If my second shot hit a Wolf, it didn't slow for a single step.

Clenching my jaw I aimed again.

Crack.

The Wolf went down and did not get up.

I didn't have a single second to celebrate my first kill.

Two more Wolves flew across the grass toward Sara, but she was so close to the tank now. The tread dug into my belly as I lay down on the tread and reached down to her. I fired another shot from that awkward position, knowing I wouldn't hit anything but hoping to give the pack pause.

Sara's hand slapped into mine and I pulled with all my strength. She clawed her way up the tread just as the closest Wolf leaped toward her. She pulled her feet up and the Wolf's jaws snapped on empty air.

CHAPTER 25

Sara panted, laying on the tank's metal tread. We were too high for the Wolves to reach us, but as the injured Wolf limped up to the pack, the two that remained were joined by four more. Seven Wolves. The same number as the pack that killed Brent. Maybe that was a common number for a Wolf pack, but I felt sure these were the same ones.

"We need to climb to the top," I urged Sara, pulling her up to a crouch.

I holstered my pistol and picked up the heavy core pack.

"You climb first," I told her and she gripped the metal rungs. It was a short distance to the top, but her strength was gone. She climbed awkwardly, her toes feeling for each rung.

When she reached the top, I followed, glad to put another few meters between us and the angry Wolf pack below us. The hatch behind the huge gun turret was closed. I hauled at the heavy latch, but three months in the damp and rain of the clearing had welded the hatch shut. It would take more than my strength to open it.

"Sit here," I told Sara and helped her rest against the back of the turret. I turned back to the Wolves.

They clicked angrily below me, circling the huge tank, sniffing the ground. The hide on their backs was nearly impervious to bullets. A thick plate of bone protected their heads, shading the shiny black eyes. The one I killed had been an exceedingly lucky shot. They were vulnerable under the neck and the belly.

Even the one I shot in the leg was not down for long. It still limped, but hardly any blood spilled from the wound. The leg was unbroken, and I thought the creature might heal before my eyes, spitting my bullet out from its shoulder like an unwanted seed in a soft fruit.

The day was young, with hours in the blazing sun before nightfall. And we hadn't lost them by traveling in the dark. I had no reason to think that waiting them out until after sunset would improve our chances. Besides, we were hardly safe on the tank. We couldn't get inside it, and if a Rex smelled us out in this field, we were done for. I had to get us out of here.

Crouching down, I counted my ammunition. Each pistol held ten rounds. I had twenty more in Sara's pack, and there were another twenty for the smaller pistol she carried. Plenty of shots. Plenty of tries to take this pack down, or at least convince them to go off in pursuit of more poorly-armed prey.

"Stay here. I'm going down where I can get a shot."

Sara's eyes opened wide and she sat up straight, grabbing my filthy shirtsleeve.

"Don't go down there. We can wait for nightfall. They'll get you if you go down there." She was almost babbling in fear and exhaustion.

"I'm not going all the way down. Just onto the treads. You

can't shoot Wolves from above," I reminded her. I peeled her hands off my leg and swung my feet over the edge of the tank. I hated turning my back on the pack, but I faced the tank as I climbed back down the rungs.

The lead Wolf was trying to climb up the treads, jumping at the heavy metal and scrambling with its front claws to get purchase. Its eyes met mine as it clawed. I expected to see hatred, feral anger, but the black hooded eyes looked as emotionless as the eyes of all its kind, darting heavy-lidded in the gray, scaled face.

I lay down on my stomach and lined up the shot. The next time the gray head appeared I squeezed the trigger, catching the wolf squarely under the jaw. It made no sound as it fell away from the tread.

"That was for Brent," I said to the still form at the foot of the tank. I took a moment to bask in the glow of the kill. I was a soldier, trained these last three years to keep my people safe in this hostile world. This was what I trained for. All the target practice, the endless drills, the months of running and climbing came down to this moment.

Two of the remaining five Wolves came around to sniff the fallen body of their leader. I sighted them down the barrel of my pistol, but I couldn't get a shot from this angle. They were too close to the tank.

I sat up, considering. My head was still on fire from the adrenaline rush of the run, the climb, the kill. My nerves were electric wires, zapping energy through my body. I pushed my sweaty hair out of my face.

The pack milled around the base of the tank, sniffing and clicking. I fired off the remaining six rounds in my pistol, hitting the Wolves closest to the tank. They danced away from the impacts, no more affected than I would be by a particularly large bloodsucker's bite. They weren't scared off, and they weren't intimidated in the slightest. And I risked alerting other predators to our location with all this gunfire.

I sat back on the tread with my back against the rungs of

the ladder. The sun beat down on my face. My nose and cheeks felt pink already. I exchanged the spent magazine for a fresh one, though I knew I could empty all my ammo into the pack's thick hides and not make a dent. I wished I could get inside the tank. One blast from the huge gun turret would surely scare this pack away. But the tank was sealed, and even if we could get inside, the missiles wouldn't fire without power.

Our lives hung by such a thin thread here, and the thread was power. The reactor core in the pack next to Sara was all that stood between Eden base and certain death. This tank had no power and so couldn't be fired to save our lives. Our own personal power was ebbing away as the sun baked us out here, exposed with no water. I shook my head, eyes closed. Thinking about water only made me thirstier.

At least I could call into base from here. The cloudless blue sky would not impede my sat trans signal. If Eden still had power, they would answer. They could send a team to pick up the power core from my coordinates. I could talk to Mom and Malia one last time. I could tell them I found Josh's tank out here. I could say goodbye.

It's better than Josh got. Or Brent, or Jack.

I pulled my trans out of my pocket and powered it up. The map it revealed showed me how far off course we were. This dead tank sat almost due north of Eden base. We were nearer the mountains than the base. I looked up toward where they rose past the trees, so close. Their brown, barren sides jutted up past the canopy, foothills of a huge, desolate range that ringed the continent.

Movement below me pulled my attention. The pack had gathered near the lifeless body of the leader. Five Wolves clicked in unison, peering intently into the tree line between the mountains and the tank.

Shots exploded out of the trees and I ducked instinctively as bullets ricocheted off the metal treads. I covered my head with my arms and pressed myself into the overgrown hull. The air was on fire with noise and smoke.

In minutes it was over. Four of the Wolf pack lay dead at the foot of the tank, while the last survivor bolted away into the forest. I lowered my arms and scanned the tree line. A lone figure strode into the clearing, empty automatic rifle smoking in the late morning heat.

It was my brother, Josh.

CHAPTER 26

I scrambled off the side of the tank, landing hard on the grass. A few of the Wolves still twitched but none got up to follow as I raced through the open field.

"Josh! Josh!" I yelled as I ran, tears half blinding me.

"Shhh! You'll draw every 'saur on the planet!" he answered, laughing. As if the explosion of gunfire wouldn't.

I plowed straight into him, knocking us both down. I hugged him as hard as I could and he hugged me back. I rolled off him and wiped my eyes on my shirtsleeves.

"You were dead," I said, and laughed.

His smile evaporated and he dropped his eyes. Deep circles ringed them, the weight of these months pressing on him.

"I know. Of course you thought I was dead. I'm so sorry. Is Mom okay? Malia?" he asked me, standing up and brushing the grass off his pants. He was filthy, but so was I.

"They were okay when I left. We've been out a while," I answered. "Where . . . where have you been? Why didn't you come home?"

Josh's shoulders sagged. He looked so much like our father now. "I couldn't," he said.

"Why not?" I asked, turning to head back toward the tank.

"Not that way," Josh said, reaching for my shoulder. "We need to get out of here. I wasn't kidding about all the 'saurs coming to the noise."

"I know, but we need to get Sara," I said.

"Sara? Our teacher, Sara? What's she doing out here?" he asked, trotting ahead of me. I quickened my pace to keep up.

"She was on the mission. Things went bad," I said, a gross oversimplification.

Sara was already climbing down off the tank when we approached. She tossed down the power core, which landed on the soft grass with a loud thump. I picked it up while she and Josh hugged a welcome. He kept an arm under Sara's shoulders as he headed back toward the trees.

"We need to go south, not north," I protested. "We have to get the core back to base." I showed Josh the power core, which he took from me and hoisted up onto his shoulders.

"Sara looks exhausted. She won't make it," Josh argued. "We'll get to safety and then make a plan from there. But we really need to get out of here now."

"I'm not sure Eden has time for that." I filled him in on what had happened at base since he disappeared. How Eden was running on the power supply from the remaining two shuttles, having lost the last of their power cores after our shuttle left.

"Your sat trans works?" Josh asked me.

"Yes. Josh, why didn't you call? Why didn't you come back? We all thought you were dead. Where is the rest of your unit?"

"No time to talk right now. The gunfire and the blood here

will draw all the scavengers."

I followed him into the forest with Sara between us. It was like having the General back again to lead the way.

"We'll get up into the hills and call from there. We have a safe place there."

"We?" I asked.

"Erik is alive, too. It's been just him and me for the last three months. He's still injured, but we found a place to hide."

I burned with a million unanswered questions, but I followed silently as he led us north, away from Eden base.

★★★

The safe place was a cave at the foot of the hillside.

We crowded inside and squeezed through a narrow passageway to a small open cavern. The entry was much too small for any of the dangerous predators to fit through. The armor plating on the Wolves' backs wouldn't let them push their way inside. I sank down onto the stone floor and felt exhaustion pull me down as the terror of the past days finally took a break. We really were safe here.

A young man sat in the middle of the cavern, tending a small fire. He looked up in surprise when we entered.

"Caleb, is that you? And who's with you? Sara? Stars, how did you ever find us?" he asked.

"I found them," Josh answered before I could speak. "Wolf pack had them cornered. I heard the shots. They were stuck on our tank in the clearing."

"Well, welcome to paradise," Erik said, indicating the dark musty cave. I smiled. After the past few days' travel, it was paradise to me.

Erik stood up. He was older than Josh but younger than Mom, and he walked over to Sara with a pronounced limp that hadn't been there when he left on the mission with Josh. "Let me get you some water and food. I can't believe you found us."

They had two of the huge water jugs from the tank, both full of fresh water. I drank greedily and so did Sara. Erik returned to the fire, and I sniffed the smoke with joy, smelling large chunks of meat cooking on a makeshift spit over the flames. Erik cracked a huge egg into a metal basin scavenged from the tank and stirred it with a stick, setting it right into the fire to cook. I was actually drooling.

We gorged on charred meat and scrambled egg. I licked the drippings off my fingers, savoring every taste.

"What happened to you guys? You look awful," Erik said around a mouthful of meat.

I shrugged. "What didn't happen to us?"

He pointed to my arms, my face. "I mean what bit you up like that?"

Sara snorted and I grinned, remembering the night I washed my pants in a flowing stream. It felt like a hundred years ago. "We found a Buzzer nest. They weren't too happy about it."

The food revived us and new energy coursed through me. Much as I hated to leave this haven, I knew we couldn't stay here.

"We need to move as soon as it's dark. Eden needs this core."

Josh looked at me across the fire. "Have you contacted them? How much time do we have?"

"No. I was about to call them when you showed up at the tank. We haven't had contact for days."

I turned on my trans but it was useless in the cave. I powered it down to conserve its remaining charge.

"I need to get up on the hill to make the call."

"Give me your trans, and I'll go in the morning," Josh offered.

"What happened to yours?" I asked him.

"Both of ours broke in the accident. We aren't even sure where we are," Erik said.

Sara's head was nodding in exhaustion. Erik pulled an emergency blanket off a pile of supplies at the back of the cave and Sara sank down gratefully.

"I'm just going to nap for a few minutes," she mumbled, laying her head on the blanket. She was asleep in seconds. She looked so comfortable.

"We need to go now," I protested to Josh. "We can't wait until morning. We need to call Eden now and leave as soon as it's dark.

We can be there by morning."

"You'll never make it, little brother," he said, shaking his head. "Look at you. You did great getting here, but you're asleep on your feet. If we leave now, you'll be a liability. And we can't climb up the mountain in the dark anyway. Sleep tonight. Tomorrow morning we'll climb up higher and use your trans to call in. Then tomorrow night we'll take the core back to base."

I shook my head again, but I was so tired. Josh's idea made sense. Surely Eden would be all right for one more day. I could sleep here tonight, in safety and comfort, and tomorrow we would head back out.

Before I went to sleep, though, I had to tell him.

"Josh, there's something you need to know."

"What's that?"

My eyes felt heavy, but my heart was heavier. "Jack was on our shuttle."

His face crumbled for a moment, deep heaving breaths racking his frame.

"Who else?" he whispered.

"Brent. Shiro. And Viktor and Raj died in the crash. Plus two of the older men and Bronton."

Josh shook his head, and murmured Jack's name.

"I'm sorry," I said. "I thought you needed to know."

He turned away from me, nodding. He did need to know. But I wish I hadn't been the one that had to tell him.

Erik handed me a blanket from the pile and I closed my eyes against the dim light of the smoldering fire. He scooted over to Josh and wrapped an arm around his shoulder. They whispered together as I fell asleep.

CHAPTER 27

I slept more soundly than I had in a week. My muscles stiffened and I woke up sore from lying still on the cave's stone floor, but as I stretched and stirred, I felt like a new man. I hadn't realized how truly exhausted I was.

Josh was awake and building up the remains of last night's fire. The small cave didn't hold on to the smoke. It drew up into invisible cracks beyond my sight in the high ceiling. There must be more caverns in this mountainside, all connected somehow for the air to circulate.

"Morning, little brother." He put some of last night's meat and some foraged greens into the metal basin and set it in the fire to cook. A real breakfast. My stomach growled audibly.

"Morning," I mumbled back.

Sara and Erik stirred at the smell of the food and soon we were all happily slurping down the stew Josh prepared.

"I didn't know you were such a great cook," I teased him.

"You make do with what you have," he smiled. "We've been out here a while. I've learned how to keep us alive." He and Erik exchanged a look.

I stood up and brushed myself off. A waft of my ripe scent hit my nostrils, and I wrinkled my nose in disgust.

"Don't guess you have a bathing tub in this palace?" I asked.

"No, but we can warm up some water and wipe you down. There are a lot of little streams that come off the high mountains, but they're way too cold for bathing," Erik said.

"Maybe we could wash our clothes, though?" Sara asked. She looked much brighter this morning, too. The solid night's sleep out of immediate danger had done us both a world of good.

"We can do that," Josh agreed.

"Later." I grabbed my trans. "We need to get out into the open somewhere and call in to base. We need to know how long they have."

Josh stood up. "Agreed. Let's climb up the mountain a bit and see what we can do."

"I'm not up for a climb," said Erik.

"I'll stay here with Erik," Sara offered. "You two go." She was eyeing the narrow passage that led outside. I could tell she didn't want to venture from the safe confines of the cave until she absolutely had to. I didn't blame her one bit.

"Okay, then. Out we go."

Josh led the way back outside. We paused at the entrance to scan the forest below us.

"Can anything climb up to here?" I asked him.

"Probably, but so far nothing has. We've been here three months, and I've never seen a big 'saur on the mountainside. There's not much up here for the grazers to eat, so I guess there's not much reason for anything to be up there. Watch out for snakes, though."

"And fliers," I added, glancing up toward the sky. We hadn't seen any since they took down our shuttle, but we'd stand out against the barren rocks of the mountainside as we climbed. I didn't relish the idea of being picked off from the sky.

We didn't talk much as we climbed. It wasn't too strenuous, but we were both paying attention to our footing. We'd get a clearer signal the higher we got and soon the forest edge was far below us. I turned on a wide ledge to look out over the treetops. Unbroken green as far as I could see. It looked like a true Eden from here, lush and fertile. In the distance, I could see the lighter patch that marked the clearing where Josh's tank rusted.

"So how did you find us?" I asked him as we resumed our climb.

"Heard the gunshots," he grunted from above me.

"How have you survived out here? And what happened to the rest of your unit?" I asked.

"Let's get up to that ledge up there. I'll tell you the whole story." The climb seemed to be wearing him out. He'd gotten soft in the past few months of hiding.

The mountainside was dry and rocky. A few small shrubs pushed through the hard dirt but it was mostly bare rock up here. We reached the ledge Josh had indicated, a wide shelf of nearly level ground that cut into the steep wall. Josh sat on a large rock, breathing hard from the effort. The sun was well up and it was already getting hot. I was sweating, but Josh was drenched.

"You're out of shape," I commented.

"Yeah," he agreed. "Haven't done much running since we found this place. It's pretty easy hunting around here, and one kill lasts us weeks. We dry out the meat over the fire."

"Let's call in to base and then you can tell me what happened." I held out my sat trans and Josh took it to place the call. He keyed in the code and waited, but no image appeared.

"We must be out of range. One of the satellites should come by at some point. We'll just have to wait until we get a signal."

I looked at the map on the trans. We didn't have contact, so it couldn't update with our current location, but the edge of the brown mountains showed up stark against all the green. I looked out over the range and saw we were on a spur that stuck out toward the south. One solid night's walking would bring us back to base. We would be there by tomorrow morning. There were isolated patches of green within the mountains' valleys to the north, but mostly these empty hills looked as dead on the map as they did in person.

I walked over to another large rock. A huge insect scuttled away as I approached and I jumped back in alarm. It had a thousand legs and a fat, brown body.

"Just a bug. Plenty of those up here. Not too bad if you cook them through," Josh laughed. I looked all around the rock before I sat down, making sure no more of those things were hiding underneath. Imagining the feeling of all those legs crawling over my skin gave me a shudder even in the baking sun. Cook them through?

"So we have the rest of the day to kill," I began. "What happened to you guys out there?"

A cloud passed over Josh's face. He began with the obvious. "Seven of us left Eden in the tank. Only Erik and I are left."

He paused and wiped his face with the tail of his shirt.

"And it was all my fault."

CHAPTER 28

Josh looked out over the unending green of the forest below us. Death lurked there unseen, death in many forms. He didn't turn to me, keeping his eyes fixed on that endless expanse as he spoke.

"We left Eden base in the morning and rode all day. The tank is really slow, so we didn't get very far. At dusk that first night, we parked and got out to do some scouting. We had a list of samples to get for the science team and we were hoping we'd find some nests. They really wanted some new Gila eggs . . . trying to make an antivenin or something. We didn't find any nests, but we got some of the plant stuff they wanted. We slept a few hours in the tank, took turns driving. We stopped again in the early morning, and then we did find some eggs. They're probably still inside the tank."

I took a drink from my canteen and offered Josh some. He sipped water and went on.

"We took turns sleeping and driving all the next day. The plan was to stop again at dusk and do some hunting, then bring the samples and the eggs and whatever meat we got straight back to base. We should have been home by the next morning. We parked the tank in that open field. It seemed awfully bright out to risk going far, but Captain Roberts wanted to get started. I didn't question him. I should have questioned him.

"I was the rear guard. We stayed together in formation, sneaking through the jungle. We all had our weapons at the ready, hoping we'd see some game. I still didn't like how light it was, but we didn't go too far from the tank. I thought it would be all right, and Roberts must have thought so, too, because he led us deeper in, until we couldn't see the tank anymore. Roberts never saw it coming. He didn't even have time to scream or shout a warning."

Josh paused. I leaned forward on the rock and waited for him to continue. I knew this story didn't have a happy ending for anyone but Josh and Erik.

"It was a Crab."

My stomach turned over. Of all the 'saurs we feared, Crabs were the most terrifying. Wolves were relentless, but they were only out in daylight. Gilas were stealthy, but if you were very careful, you could usually stay out of their range. Distraction near a Gila was fatal, as the General learned too late, but they hadn't killed very many of us in our time on this planet. T-rex was a monster, but you could hear it coming, and try to hide or get up a tree. But Crabs were invisible.

We named them after something that used to live in Earth's oceans, some kind of bottom-dwelling scuttler that had a hard shell. One kind of Earth crab would stick stuff to the back of its shell to disguise itself, so when it sat still, it just looked like any other bit of the sea floor. For the Earth crabs, it was a matter of defense. But Eden Crabs were pure predator.

Bigger than Gilas, smaller than Brachis, they had thick

armored plates that overlapped across their heads and backs. They rolled in the dirt to coat themselves with soil and then waited for Eden's plant life to take over. By the time they were adults, they were so grown-over with vines and plants that even a Wolf wouldn't notice them. The plants on their armor attracted the same bugs as all the other ferns, so they had the same phosphorescence. In the dark, they glowed just like everything else around them. And they were big enough to stay active at night, especially since their hunting strategy required just one single movement. They waited, still and silent, with their huge heads on the ground. When some unsuspecting 'saur—or human—got close enough . . . one chomp from those jaws could break a Brachi's leg. Or cut a human in half. I shuddered. Roberts probably never even knew what killed him.

"Crabs are usually solitary," Josh continued. "I knew not to shoot. It was too late for Roberts; he was dead before he hit the ground. And the Crab wasn't going to go after anyone else. It had its meal right there. I knew the rules. If it's Wolves, shoot. If it's Gilas, Rexes, or Crabs, run. But my hand was on my gun and my finger was on the trigger and I didn't even mean to shoot, but I just unloaded into the Crab. I stood there and shot every single round in my automatic right into the thing's head. Dirt and leaves flew off it everywhere, but it just dropped its head and closed its eyes and took it. Didn't even shake its head or anything, just waited for me to run out of ammo. Then it opened its eyes and swallowed what was left of Roberts in two gulps."

I was sweating. I could hear the shots, feel the whoosh of bullets flying. If I'd been there, I would have run. But Josh stood his ground and fired.

"Everyone else ran like they should have. I realized how stupid I'd been. I stopped to reload, then took off after them. That kind of noise is a magnet. We had to get back to the tank."

Josh blinked hard, squinting into the sun. His eyes were watering, whether from the blinding glare or from the memory, I wasn't sure.

"We almost made it. The Wolves must have been really close

to get to us so fast."

He didn't need to continue. I knew what a Wolf pack could do to men who had nowhere to run.

"It's okay," I said, but he cut me off.

"I was the last one because I'd stopped to reload. That's why I'm alive. They came from ahead of us, running through that field. It was just chaos. Everybody was shooting, just firing at anything that moved. I couldn't see far enough through the trees to know what I was aiming at. We got some of them."

He wiped his nose on his shirtsleeve and took another drink. I didn't interrupt him.

"When it was all over, when all the shooting stopped, there were five dead Wolves. And four dead men. There wasn't much left of any of them. When I got to the worst of it, it was . . . I can't even describe it. Blood everywhere . . . Wolf blood and human. Bodies all over. I thought I was the only survivor. But then I heard a noise, someone moaning in pain. Erik was pinned under a dead Wolf. I rolled the thing off him and helped him up. I knew we had to get out of there. I didn't know how many Wolves had been in the pack, whether any of them were still out there."

"Why didn't you just get back in the tank and drive it home?" I asked.

"Maybe I should have. I was just in shock, I guess. But it was still way too bright out. The tank was on the other side of that open field and I just . . . couldn't walk out into that open space. I knew they'd be on me if I did. Maybe they would have. Maybe they should have."

He paused again.

"Erik was pouring blood out of a wound in his leg. It was getting dark and I just carried him through the jungle. I didn't know where I was going. I was still on fire from the attack. I just moved, trying to get as far away from all that death as I could. So stupid. But after what seemed like forever, I found myself climbing up this hill and the forest fell away behind me. I was mostly dragging Erik by that point. I found this cave and pulled him inside where we both collapsed."

Josh continued.

"Eventually I got myself together. I scavenged some wood from near the cave opening, enough to get a fire going. I had some water in my canteen and I started checking over Erik's wounds. There were just two big punctures in his leg, and at first I thought they were bite wounds. But as I cleaned them out I realized they were bullet holes."

CHAPTER 29

I slapped at a swarm of little flying insects that were drawn to my sweaty face. Josh didn't say anything for a few minutes, lost in the memory.

"But you saved him. You got him out of there and up here to where it's safe. You saved Erik's life."

Josh turned to look at me then, the first time since he began the awful story. The look he had on his face haunts me still.

"If not for me, they would all still be alive. I'm the one who shot at the Crab. I drew the Wolf pack. And I might have even been the one that shot Erik, who knows? It was such a mess, I didn't even know what I was shooting at. I might have shot him."

"Maybe," I agreed. "But listen. You think a Wolf pack that

close to you didn't already know you were there? Yeah, you shot at the Crab, but really, you think those Wolves would have just passed you by? They were already tracking you. They knew where you were. You said it yourself, they came from ahead of you as you were running back to the tank. They were on your trail before you ever fired at the stupid Crab. If you hadn't done that, you'd still have been the rear guard when they attacked you from behind. You would have been the first to go down and nobody would have even turned around in time. Every one of you would have died."

Josh blinked at me. He looked like he wanted to believe what I just said. He dropped his eyes and shook his head.

"No, they wouldn't. Maybe they would have got me. But then the guys in the front . . . Bradley and Jason . . . they would have maybe gotten away."

"Maybe. But you and Erik would be dead. Look, either way you weren't all coming back from that mission. Captain Roberts took you out too early. The Wolves were still hunting. And you just did like he ordered you, you all did. And it cost the other guys their lives. But you saved Erik and you saved yourself. Who else could have done that?"

He kicked the dirt at the base of the rock, digging a little V in the dry sand with his boot heel.

I waited for him to respond. Finally he looked me in the eyes.

"I'm not sure you're right, little brother. But thanks. I guess I look a lot better through your eyes."

I swallowed the lump that formed in my throat.

"You're a hero. You saved Erik's life, and you saved me and Sara back at the tank. If you hadn't been there . . ." I let the thought trail off.

"Me? You're the hero. You carried that damned heavy power core through this jungle all by yourself. You never gave up even when it was just you and the teacher. Sara never would have made it without you. And when we get that core back to base they're going to rename it 'Caleb City' after the kid who saved what's left of the human race."

I smiled. "Hardly. But you're right. When we get the core

back, everything will be okay."

Josh squinted up into the sky. "Let's try the call again."

He handed me the sat trans and I punched in the code. There was static, then a voice on the other end.

"Hello? General Carthage, is that you?"

"No, sir. It's Caleb and Josh Wilde reporting."

"Caleb? And Josh? Hang on, boy, I'm going to send for your mother."

I turned to Josh.

"It's Enrico. He's going to get mom. She's going to freak out." I smiled at the thought. On the other end I could hear her screaming through the static. She came on the line breathless.

"Josh? Is that you? Caleb?"

"It's me, Mom," I said. "And Josh is here. He's okay. And Sara is with us, and Erik's alive, too. But that's all." I thought she might ask about the General, but she was too overjoyed about Josh and me being alive to register what I'd said.

"Where are you? What happened? I need to talk to Josh!" I handed him the trans.

His shoulders started to shake as they talked. He turned away from me, didn't want me to see him cry. I didn't know how much he'd tell her, but I wanted to give him some privacy.

I shuffled over to the side of the ledge we had perched on. I craned my neck, looking up at the walls of rock on either side. In the overhang above me I saw a shadow, a wide open hole in the stone. There were some large, loose boulders and dead shrubs underneath the opening, as if a recent rain had dislodged them and revealed the tunnel. It was just a little ways up from where we were sitting. Josh was still talking on the trans, whether to Mom or to Enrico now, I wasn't sure. I looked back up at that inviting opening, and the promise of shade inside.

It was a short climb to the hole in the wall. The mouth of the cave was tall and wide and it opened onto a large empty chamber. My flashlight was hooked to my belt. I aimed the beam around to make sure nothing was hiding inside, but Josh was right that none of the 'saurs were inclined to climb up here. The cave smelled musty and my footsteps echoed as I stepped inside. Passages led off the main chamber to the right and left.

I'll just look in a little ways. Just stay out of Josh's hair for a few minutes. Just see what's down this way.

The right hand passage narrowed until I had to stoop over, then squat, then crawl. I hoped it might open up farther on, but it got tight enough that I was afraid I might get stuck if I went any farther. I backed out until I could turn around, then retraced my steps to the larger cavern. I peeked out the opening and down. Josh was still talking to Eden base.

He shouldn't use up all the charge, I thought, but didn't say it. He hadn't talked to Mom for three months. They must have had a lot to say.

The left passage started out smaller than the right but stayed open enough that I could walk upright. It quickly got dark as the tunnel twisted and turned through the rock. My flashlight threw jagged shadows on the walls.

I stumbled as the passage ended abruptly in a wide, empty space. My light couldn't reach the far walls of this cave but I didn't need it anyway. The ceiling was hung with stalactites, each one encrusted with tiny worms that glowed with their own blue light. The whole place looked like the night sky, blue stars twinkling high overhead. The beauty of it took my breath and for a few minutes I stood silently, thinking about a planet that held such danger and such glorious wonder.

Josh has to see this, I thought, and turned to head back up the passage. I switched on my flashlight for the walk through the dark passage, and its beam hit the wall through which I had just arrived. And on that wall, I saw the writing.

CHAPTER 30

I played my flashlight over the rough walls of the cave.

It really was writing.

Not some kind of debris left by crawling insects, or some random pattern from centuries of water trickling down from the glowing ceiling, but intricate shapes painted in straight vertical lines as far as my beam illuminated. I had no idea what it said, and didn't recognize a single letter or number. It looked like nothing I'd ever seen in the enormous archives of Horizon's stored history of all Earth's written works. Asian characters and Middle Eastern letters, ancient Greek and even hieroglyphics . . . I couldn't read a word of them, but I knew what they looked like.

These lines were straight and scratchy, with lots of parallels and crosshatching. The paint flaked in places, but it didn't look ancient. I followed the wall of writing around the perimeter of the room and made another discovery. Of the many passages that led off this huge cave, only some were natural. The tunnel I had walked through to get here, that led back out to the front opening of the mountain where Josh waited for me, that one was a rough channel of varying height and width. Several other natural holes led off this space, but others had the rounded smoothness that only fine tools could shape. Flat floors and clear cuts told me these tunnels were not formed by water or by the natural movement of continents that pushed mountains up from the sea and rent holes in stone.

Someone lives here. Someone that isn't a 'saur or a dumb shrew.

I racked my brain, remembering all I'd been taught about Earth animals. There had been plenty of diggers, creatures who burrowed into the soil to make safe nests or hunt for prey. Even worms could push through softer dirt. Could an animal have carved these rounded spaces?

The blue light from the cave ceiling and my flashlight's thin beam did not illuminate this space to my liking. My imagination went wild in the dark, enclosed space.

I had watched too many movies onboard Horizon. An image of horror popped into my brain, of giant worms that bored through the ground. That could bore through solid stone, just like this, on a planet far from Earth. I pictured huge worms with gnashing teeth, spiraling through solid rock toward me from every side. It was just a movie. Not real. They couldn't know if it was real. Or maybe enormous moles with steel claws, scrabbling through the mountain to investigate this noise, this human smell. Who or what had carved these passages, and where were they now?

The hairs on the back of my neck stood up in primal dread.

Stop it. You're being ridiculous. This isn't Dune. I kept my back pressed to the wall, wildly swinging my flashlight through the darkness. Inching around to the path I had entered by, I gritted my teeth, waiting for claws or teeth to rip through the stone and my body. But nothing moved in this gloom except me and the tiny glowing worms that twinkled on the ceiling. When I reached the correct tunnel I ran, ducking and weaving around the natural rock formations that suddenly looked so comforting.

I emerged blinking from the mouth of the cave.

"Josh! Scat it, Josh, you have to see this!" I shouted down to him.

He stood up, tucking my trans into his pocket. "Where did you get off to? I was getting worried."

"Never mind that, Josh, you have got to see what's in this cave!" I repeated. I felt much braver in the sunlight.

"Okay, what did you find? Let's be quick about it. We have a long walk tonight."

"Come up here. I can't tell you, you just need to see it."

He frowned and looked out across the jungle. The sun was nearing its zenith. If we were going to try to reach base tonight, we had about seven hours before we needed to leave. Plenty of time.

I led him down the left-hand tunnel and into the huge open cave.

"Whoa, this is really beautiful," he began, looking up at the indoor sky of blue glowing stars.

"Not that," I said, grabbing his shoulders to turn him back toward the wall. "This."

He didn't say anything for a moment.

"This looks like writing."

"That's what I thought. It's paint. See? It's flaking off in places, you can pick it away. No way is it natural." I took his arm and pulled him down the wall. "That's not all, though. Look at this," I said, and played my flashlight beam around the smooth edge of one of the unnatural tunnels.

"You know what this means?" he asked quietly, running his hands over the tool marks on the wall.

"Something else lives here. Something that's not a 'saur."

"Something intelligent, that uses tools and paint," he added.

"Are you sure? Could it be some kind of huge tunneling animal?" I asked. The gaping maw of my imaginary tunnel worm flashed into my mind.

"No, I don't think so. These marks are too regular, too smooth. No animal did this. It looks like the work of humans, but you and I are the first to ever set foot in this place. And the painting on the wall, whatever those letters are. Not an animal, definitely."

I nodded in the blue worms' glow.

"Sara has got to see this. She'll go nuts."

Josh laughed. "That's for sure. I'm not sure Erik can make the climb up here, but let's go tell them."

I followed him back out of the cave.

"So what did Mom say? How long do they have at base? We're going tonight?" In the excitement of discovery I had almost forgotten about Eden base.

"Their power is getting low. They can hold out through tomorrow as long as nothing presses the fence."

I stopped smiling. When one of the bigger 'saurs bumped into the electric wires surrounding our base, the current gave it a nasty jolt. But it often caused a power surge through the fence. With only the fading power supply from the two remaining shuttles, Eden's fences wouldn't survive a large surge. And once the 'saurs figured out the wires weren't juiced anymore . . .

"So we go tonight, right? We can make it by morning. Once the power core is installed, everyone will be okay."

"We go tonight," Josh agreed. "And the core will hold us for a while."

CHAPTER 31

Sara went nuts.

"Writing? Real writing, not just mold or something on the cave walls? You're sure?"

She peppered us with questions as we repeated the morning's climb. Erik stayed below. I hoped he'd be able to keep up tonight on the way back to base. The bullets were probably still in his leg somewhere, but the wounds had closed over in the three months he and Josh had been hiding in the lower cave.

We brought all the flashlights and a large lantern, part of the haul Josh had recovered from the tank. The back of the small cave below held weapons and ammo, blankets and medical supplies.

"Why didn't you just get in the tank and drive Erik back to

base?" I asked Josh as we climbed.

"I tried to. But we left the hatch open when we went out on the mission and by the time I got back to the tank, the shrews had gotten inside. They must have chewed through some wiring or something because it doesn't start."

My heart sank. For a brief moment I pictured us crashing through the forest in that tank tonight, rumbling along with the power core safely stowed away. I wasn't able to open the hatch when I was alone on the tank, but I hoped maybe Josh and I together could have popped it. Figures it wouldn't work. It looked like we would be walking after all. As much as I hated the idea of trudging through the jungle again, I felt a moment's relief. If the tank had been working, Josh could have come back to Eden base at any time. As thrilled as I was to find him out here, I couldn't help feeling a tiny bit of resentment that we'd mourned him for months while he hid in a cave.

We reached the entrance to the cavern. Sara plunged ahead, eager to get to the writings.

"Take the left-hand passage," I called to her as she disappeared into the darkness.

I heard her exclaim when she got to the huge glowing chamber.

"Amazing! It's glowworms up there!"

Josh and I exchanged a grin.

Sara was kneeling on the floor examining the first column of strange writing when we emerged. The large lantern lit most of the cave and I could now see to the far walls. Maybe ten passages led away from this enormous hall, most of them smooth and round.

I walked into the middle of the room with far more confidence than the first time I was here.

"I'm going to check out some of these tunnels," I said, and chose one at random.

It led off to the right, deep into the mountainside. I crept along until I came to an opening, another passage leading off at a right angle. I considered following it, but decided that since I had no string or paint to mark my way, I should stay on the straight path. Even with Josh and Sara within shouting distance, I didn't want to get lost in what might be a confusing warren of tunnels.

Several more paths led away from this main thoroughfare, but I continued until it dead-ended in a T. I chose the left-hand fork. I'll just see what's down here. But there were more passages leading into this one, and I knew I'd lose my way in no time, so I retraced my steps to the huge open room where Sara was frantically scribbling in her sketchbook. I didn't see Josh.

"There are tunnels and more tunnels in this place," I said.

Sara looked up from her writing.

"Someone cut these tunnels," she said, echoing my earlier thought.

"Do you think they're still here?" I asked her.

"I don't think so. Not for a long time. Ours are the only footprints in the dirt, and this paint is old. It doesn't look like anyone has been here in many years."

I nodded. "That's what I thought, too. It just feels abandoned. It reminds me of Horizon, how it must look inside now." My father and a few of his officers stayed behind in the chaos of the evacuation. The oxygen wouldn't have lasted more than a few hours once the ship's hull was breached by the explosion that sent us fleeing for the planet's surface. It would be dark in there now, airless, still. Only ghosts prowled its metal hallways, silent in endless orbit.

"I agree," Sara said. "I wonder who these people were? And where they went?"

"Can you read any of the writing?"

"No. It's nothing like I've ever seen before. I don't know the characters or the language it's written in. But you were right, someone here had a lot to say."

"Where did Josh go?"

"Exploring, like you. He said we could spend an hour here, then we should try to get a nap in before sundown." Her face darkened.

"Just one more night in the jungle," I encouraged her. "By morning we'll be home."

"Home," she repeated, and turned back to the markings on

the wall.

I chose a different tunnel at the far end of the cavern. This one was smaller. At regular intervals small chambers branched off it, single rooms hewn out of the stone. Most of them were empty, but a few held objects I couldn't identify. Some of it resembled furniture, wooden pallets that might have once been padded with cloth or woven grass to make a mattress. Tiny items of bright metal, some of it still bearing vividly-colored paint were under the pallet, as if left behind and forgotten by whoever lived here once. I picked one of the little metal things up. It was a clip of some kind, hinged to clamp on top of something. No rust marred its surface and the front was painted in red and gold in a swirling pattern. I tucked it into my pocket.

A recent memory flashed into my mind as I tucked the bright metal object away. A memory of the General digging around the mud of the swamp, excavating another shining metal object. Whoever painted on these walls and made the discarded items I was seeing in the tunnels, they had traveled as far as the swamp. Or had some kind of drone that traveled for them.

The hallway ended in a steep staircase leading downward. There were no handrails, and my flashlight didn't penetrate far into the gloom. I listened and heard nothing moving below but a breath of moving air fluttered past my face.

I turned back at the top of the stairs.

On the way down this hallway I had looked into the rooms on the left side. Now I reversed direction, looking at the rooms on the other side. I kept flashing my light behind me, making sure nothing had crept up those dark stairs, but I was alone.

The last room I examined was the closest to the cave where Sara worked. It was larger than the others and I shined my light along the walls.

It was full of paintings, pictures drawn in the same paint as the writing in the main cavern. They showed figures with two legs and two arms, figures that walked upright like humans. The shapes didn't look human, but there was no question that the posture was bipedal. I moved along, examining the pictures. I saw the images of the painters, which I assumed these figures depicted, engaged in different activities. One picture clearly showed a T-rex eating one of the humanoids. One showed a Wolf pack. And one of them clearly showed a circle of them around a Brachi lying on the ground . . . a successful hunt. My flashlight showed these images, one by one.

I was so engrossed in the pictures that until I tripped over it, I didn't even notice the body.

CHAPTER 32

I yipped and jumped back.

But there was no mistaking what it was. My mouth hung open as I stared at it.

It was ages dead, dried and shriveled. Tight skin stretched over bones, flesh mummified by the dry air in the cave.

I backed out of the room and ran for the light of the lantern.

"Sara! Josh!" I yelled, skidding to a halt in the middle of the huge cave.

"What are you yelling about? You'll wake the dead!" Josh joked, emerging from a nearby tunnel.

"I won't wake this dead," I answered. "Come here, both of you. There's one of them still here!"

"One of who?" Josh asked.

I led them to the room and shined my light on the desiccated corpse.

"Stars," Sara murmured.

Illuminated by all three of our flashlights, the still form looked less alarming.

"It looks . . . like a bird." Sara said.

And it did. The figures painted on the wall with their strangely-shaped heads and long arms suddenly made sense. The mummy lay curled on the floor. Its two empty eye sockets sat atop a rounded beak with teardrop nostrils and a serrated edge. Its two legs ended in taloned feet that were flat on the bottom. The creature wore a rotted garment long-stripped of color, and the skin of its head and long arms were studded with the decayed pins of what must once have been feathers. One long-fingered hand rested on a metal dish, black with the dried remains of his paint.

"It doesn't make any sense," Sara murmured.

"Look at the pictures," I said, shining my light on the walls of this room. Each picture was accompanied by writing in the same scratchy characters as the main cave. Sara examined one of the drawings.

"It's obvious that his kind drew these," she said. "Look, you can see the beak and the . . . wings? Arms?"

"They walked on two legs like us," Josh said.

"And none of these drawings show them flying," she agreed. "But that's not what is so strange. Have you seen any birds here on Eden? Ever?"

"Well, the pterosaurs fly like birds," I offered.

"Yes, but they're not birds. I mean like Earth birds. With feathers. Like this guy," she indicated the still mummy on the floor.

"No. I only know real birds from books."

"Exactly. So what is he doing here? If this planet evolved birds smart enough to have written language and tools, then where are the rest? Not just where are the rest of this poor fellow's lost tribe, but where are the other branches of the family? Earth was full of primates, of which humans were the smartest. So where are all the other species of birds?"

None of us had an answer.

Sara knelt down next to the mummy.

"We can't stay here," I said. "We need to get back down the mountain and get geared up. We have to leave for base in a few hours."

Sara looked stricken. "I can't leave now. I have to study this. I need to record all these drawings, the writing. I need to study the body."

"We need to get the power core back to Eden. Otherwise we'll be the only four people left alive on the planet," I reminded her.

"Or the only four people left alive in the universe," Josh said, almost to himself. It was a sobering thought.

"Maybe so, if we don't hurry," I insisted.

Sara hesitated and opened her mouth as if to protest, then followed us out of the small room.

We collected the lantern and climbed back down to the lower cave where Erik waited. We told him all about our finds, and he nodded in wonder.

"Where did they go? Maybe they're still here on the planet somewhere. Maybe they could help us."

Sara shook her head. "That cave has been abandoned for years, maybe centuries. I don't know how long it takes for a body to dry out like that, but no one has been in these caves for a very long time. I doubt there are any bird people left here."

I took the power core out of the tattered pack and placed it in a newer one, cinching down the flap. I started to organize the weapons Josh had salvaged from the tank.

"We'll make a travel pack for each of us. Weapons and flashlights," I began.

"I'm not going," Sara said.

"What?" I asked, confused.

"I'm staying here. I can't leave this place. I need to study it, figure out what happened here. I can't go back to Eden now." Her eyes were pleading but her lips were set in a straight line.

"I'll stay with Sara," Erik said.

Josh whipped his head around to look at Erik.

"You can't stay. Neither of you can stay. We're going back to base together and that's that. Once the base is secure, you can come back here with a science team and study that dead bird all you want."

Sara crossed her arms across her chest.

"That will never happen. Once we get back to base we'll hunker down behind our fences and hide like shrews in a woodpile. They'll never risk a shuttle to come back here. And when this power core runs out? Then what?" Her eyes dropped to the ground. "Then we die, that's what." She shook her head. "One power core between what's left of the human race and certain death? No way, not me. We're just buying time and you know it."

I had never heard her so vehement before. In a way, she was right; we were just buying time. But it was time we could use to think of another plan, find another source of power. Time was the only thing we could buy, and I told her so.

"They're counting on us. We're not going to sit here in this little cave while the lights go out and the fences go down around our people. We have to try."

Her face crumbled.

"Of course you have to try. You and Josh take the core back to base. Erik and I will stay here and move up to the upper cave. Maybe I can learn something that will help us survive."

"It didn't help the bird people," I said, and then wished I hadn't. Hope was all we had left.

"No, it didn't. But it's all I can do. I can't go out there again."

I understood then. She had lost hope that she would live to reach Eden. Somehow the idea of drying up in the cave next to the ancient bird mummy appealed to her more than being eaten by a hungry 'saur in the jungle.

I bowed my head in resignation. "You're right. You and Erik should stay here. Josh and I will go alone."

CHAPTER 33

We walked in silence, feeling the weight of the gloomy forest pressing on us. I hadn't realized until we crept back under the canopy of leaves how free I had felt in the open air on the mountain. I was born on a ship rocketing through space. My first taste of non-recycled air was tainted by fear of the huge predators we had landed among. Eden base sat in a clearing next to a wide flowing river, but I never knew the exhilaration of breathing deeply with my face turned toward the sun until I sat on the bare rocks of the dry hillside.

I understood what Sara meant. I didn't want to leave those caves, either. But my mother and Malia and a hundred other people were counting on Josh and me to bring back this power core and hope of survival.

We left the sat trans with Sara at the cave. It wouldn't work in the heavy jungle anyway, and Eden knew to expect us just before dawn. We wouldn't be able to signal our impending arrival, but we hoped to enter the gate before the sun rose. Captain Enrico— maybe General Enrico now, I thought with a sourness in my stomach—would be waiting to open the gate as soon as he saw us. It was a primitive system, and we had to shut off the electricity to the fence-line to open either the large gate through which our tanks rolled or the small human-sized portal just next to it.

Josh had a better sense of direction than I did. He tracked through the forest like one born to it, and I followed, pistol drawn. As the night cooled and the air filled with the familiar songs of the little 'saurs in the trees, we both relaxed a bit. No Wolves would be out now, no Gilas awake. There were still dangers, but for the first time since we lost General Carthage, I dared to hope we might actually succeed.

"So how's Mom?" I asked. Josh had spent a long time talking with her on the trans while I explored the birdman's caves above him. I hadn't asked him about the conversation.

"She's all right. She could barely talk she was so glad to hear from me. I'm really sorry I put her through that, thinking I was dead. It must have been awful for her."

"It was. She said that now you were gone, she would never see dad's face again. She hadn't mentioned him at all since we left Horizon. But you do look like him."

"A little," he agreed. "Dad was . . . a great man." He swallowed hard.

"I remember. I wonder how long he survived after the transports blasted off. I wonder if he knew we landed safely before he died."

Josh didn't answer.

"But then 'safely' isn't really how we landed."

"No, it wasn't. But we've done all right here. There's still enough of us. If we're careful and lucky, we might survive here."

"Do you really think so?" I asked in a small voice. Sara's words were haunting me. The core we carried would buy us time, but would it be enough?

"I have to think so," Josh said, snapping me out of my reverie. "Otherwise it's all for nothing."

We slogged through the jungle in silence once more.

Hours into the journey we paused to eat some dried meat and drink from our canteens. I still had mine, and it felt like a talisman in my hands. The letters "C. Wilde" were scratched into its metal surface and I rubbed them absently with my finger as I drank.

"So what's the plan when we get there?" I asked.

"We shouldn't need much of a plan," Josh answered. "There's not much open space between the edge of the jungle and the postern gate," he named the smaller human-sized entrance. "As long as we're clear, we'll just run across the field. They'll be watching for us and open the gate when we get there."

Again, I dared to hope. We were so close now.

We pushed on through the darkest part of the night. The blue-green glow of the phosphorescent leaves allowed us to travel without our flashlights on. We moved quickly and deliberately, pausing only when some movement or noise made us freeze, listening.

I was bone weary. Last night's deep sleep had restored me, but the week of terrifying travel that preceded it were catching up again. We had planned to nap in the afternoon, but our discovery in the caves took all day. The pack of weapons on my back felt heavier with each step I took. It was getting harder and harder to pick my feet up, and I stumbled over roots and downed branches.

"We're almost there. You can sleep for a week once we get inside the fence," Josh said, noticing my fatigue.

"That sounds amazing," I mumbled.

The hours passed in a blur, as I dragged myself through the darkness. Even the bloodsuckers' sharp stings failed to rouse me from my plodding stupor. I longed to rest, to sit on the moist ground and pillow my head on some gnarled root. But that would be an invitation for the flesh-boring worms to creep from the soil and tunnel right into my skin, and that would mean months of agony as they chewed away my flesh from the inside. The thought kept me moving.

Josh stopped suddenly and I walked right into his back. He didn't speak, just caught me with one arm. I blinked my eyes open and stood beside him.

"What is it?" I whispered.

The glow of pre-dawn had crept through the forest as I walked, unseeing. It wasn't anywhere near full light yet, but I could begin to see farther through the forest. The glowing leaves were losing the night's phosphorescence, and mist was rising from the ground. Everything looked gray and blurry. I rubbed my eyes, leaving them closed for a moment longer than I needed to.

"We're almost there. Time to look alive."

I sipped from my canteen to wake myself up, splashing some water on my face.

"I don't see the lights yet," I said. Eden base stayed lit all night, a warning to any inquisitive 'saurs that the fence was live.

"We're not close enough for that. But soon. Let's move."

I focused on Josh's back and stepped forward.

Through my soggy boots I felt the unmistakable tremor shiver through the ground. Somewhere nearby, a T-rex was hunting.

CHAPTER 34

My eyes popped open, fatigue burning off in an instant of electric recognition.

We didn't speak, just crouched down where we were. One footfall didn't let us pinpoint the Rex's location. We waited for it to move again.

There.

Vibration shuddered through the forest. The Rex was somewhere ahead and to our left. The smaller 'saurs fell silent at the predator's approach and the rushing sound of water whispered in the sudden quiet.

"The river," I whispered right into Josh's ear. "We're almost there."

He nodded. We scuttled low through the brush, my aching thighs protesting the movement. I took Josh's arm and pointed to a nearby tree with good low branches. Should we climb? I pantomimed.

He shook his head and continued toward our destination, veering to the right, away from the sound of the Rex and toward the noise of the river.

The forest around us brightened as we scrambled. Just ahead, a huge tree had recently fallen. Its leaves hung limp on the branches as the uprooted base grasped at the air. It left a gaping hole in the dirt, and we ducked under the archway beneath the huge downed trunk.

I wriggled underneath it and peeked through the weedy shrubs. Gray mist still obscured my vision and dawn had yet to fully break, but ahead and below me I saw the most welcome of sights: the lights of Eden glowed in the river valley before us.

"We're here," I whispered.

"I know."

"And we're not too late. There are still lights on."

He squinted through the mist.

"Not all of them. It should be brighter than that."

"So they're conserving power. It's okay, we've got the core." I patted the heavy pack Josh carried. "What are we waiting for?" We were in sight of our target. I could practically hear their welcoming shouts.

"We have to wait for the mist to burn off. Didn't you hear the Rex?"

Of course I heard the Rex.

"We can just run," I said recklessly. But if the Rex's heat-sensors picked us up, we'd be its breakfast. Neither of us could outrun a Rex on open ground, and until the mist lifted, running would be foolish. And Eden wouldn't be able to see us coming to shut down the fence power and let us in.

My hands shook with impatience. Eden base was right down the hill. Just a sprint away.

The first rays of true dawn broke through the jungle. We

crouched under the fallen tree and waited for the morning mist to evaporate.

A few more of Eden's lights winked out.

"They're running low. We need to get down there." I fidgeted in the gloom.

"I know. But it's for nothing if we don't make it in."

The tree above us vibrated with the Rex's heavy tread. We pressed our backs into the muddy roots. It was close.

Tense minutes passed. The mist began to lift. I peeked back under the tree and down the hill.

Eden still had a few lights on, a good sign. Squinting into the distance, I could begin to make out movement inside the fences, tiny people moving around between the hulking shapes of our downed transports and shuttles.

And between our hiding place at the edge of the forest and the closed gates of Eden, two Rexes waited.

Their backs were to Josh and me as they watched the people of Eden, drawn by the heat of their bodies and the smell of their meat. They kept back from the fence-line, obviously familiar with the jolt of the wires. I could see their huge chests expand as they inhaled, smelling the warm scent of humans.

"Two Rexes," I whispered to Josh. He nodded beside me.

Eden's power was almost gone. If one of them pressed the fence and took the charge, the surge would spark out the rest of the fence. The other Rex would snap through the wires like strands of spider web. The Rexes couldn't know how close they were to wiping out our base, but we did. And the people inside the fences certainly did, too.

"We have to draw them away from the gate," Josh said. He opened the weapons pack.

"Do we have anything we can launch? A handheld to scare them off?" We had precious few hand-launched rockets, but they made an enormous explosion when they detonated. It might not kill a Rex, but a direct hit would surely send the pair off in search of easier prey.

"No. We have a couple of grenades and plenty of rounds for

the guns."

Our bullets were useless against Rex hide. When we shot at them, they just stamped their huge feet, barely annoyed by the little stings of our automatic rifles.

Josh came to a decision.

"I'll head around to the side and draw them away. You take the core and run for the gate."

His words were a punch in the stomach. "No way," I protested. "We have to stay together."

"We can't. If they press the fence now, it's all over. I'll head through the tree line with the grenades." He pointed away from the river, where the open field was wider. "I'll toss them out, make a big bang. They'll chase me and I'll lead them into the trees. You'll have a clear sprint."

I shook my head. My throat felt tight. "I'll do it. I'm a better climber than you. I can get up a tree faster. You take the core in."

"You're also a faster runner. If either of us has any chance to get this core in, it's you and you know it."

I bit my lip. Josh was right. If it came down to speed, I was the obvious choice. But I had lost Josh once. I couldn't bear the thought of losing him again, not when we were so close.

"Isn't there any other way?" I asked.

He smiled, and his eyes were moist.

"You carried the core all this way. You'll make it through that gate. I know you can do it."

He put his hands on my shoulders and looked into my eyes. "If I don't make it back, tell Mom I love her and I'm sorry."

I gritted my teeth. "You'll make it. Get up a tree as soon as you get the Rexes on the move. Get up high. We'll send out a tank to chase them away from you." I was babbling like a child. Josh knew what to do.

"I will," he promised. He loaded the grenades onto his belt and took the automatic rifle.

"Here." He handed me a pair of binoculars from the pack. "Watch me until I get over there," he pointed to the edge of the trees far away from the gates. "When I pass that big rock, get ready to run. As soon as the Rexes move, you go."

I shook my head, but he smiled and clapped me on the shoulder.

"Goodbye, Caleb."

I clutched his arm and said nothing. In a moment, I let him go.

CHAPTER 35

I picked up the binoculars. It was nearly full light now, and I had no trouble following his progress even through the heavy tree cover. The Rexes were still prowling near the gate. I put down the binoculars long enough to hitch the power core pack onto my shoulders. When I picked them up again, I couldn't see Josh anymore.

I scanned the edge of the tree line, looking for movement.

There. A tiny movement in the bushes.

I focused in. It wasn't Josh.

Maybe just wind in the branches, I thought, and focused closer. There it was again, the tiniest movement. I only saw it because I was looking right at it.

My mouth went dry and my legs felt weak underneath me as I panned the focus down to where the bushes met the grass. I stared for a long moment, needing to be certain.

A black shiny bead was almost hidden in the still shrubbery. And as I watched it, ever so slowly, it blinked.

I dropped the binoculars in the mud.

"Crab!" I shouted, but Josh couldn't hear me over the morning songs of the forest. The Rexes cocked their heads, listening, then turned back to watch the people of Eden, so nearly in their reach.

I snatched the binoculars up again and my hands shook as I panned down the tree line. I found Josh's moving form after a moment's panicked searching. He was heading straight for the Crab.

He'd never see it. They were so perfectly camouflaged, so still. You never saw one until it had you. He wouldn't live long enough to get off a shot or toss a grenade. And he would die for nothing.

I didn't think. I stood up from the sheltering tree and fired four shots straight up into the air.

The Rexes whipped their heads around to stare in my direction. The tree hid my silhouette but they sniffed the air and crouched down to spring in my direction. The forest was silent.

Josh burst out of the tree line. I could hear him shouting in the distance.

BOOM.

The first grenade exploded and the Rexes turned toward it. Josh sprinted through the field. I couldn't see the Crab at this distance, but Josh was no longer heading towards it, cutting diagonally across the clearing, waving his arms and yelling.

The Rexes couldn't resist. They charged around the fence-line, heads low and arms grasping forward. Josh tossed another grenade toward them.

BOOM. Dirt sprayed up from the explosion, but the Rexes didn't slow. Josh angled back toward the tree line.

I tore my eyes away from the retreating figure of my brother. The moment had arrived.

I sprinted down the hill.

My pulse pounded in my head as I ran headlong through the open field. My lungs felt heavy as I sucked in the humid air.

Ahead of me the postern gate opened, and armed men burst through. A shot whizzed by my head and I stumbled in shock. Why were they shooting at me? Couldn't they see who I was?

I tripped and fell, skidding on my belly with the heavy pack crushing my ribcage. I rolled on my side, lying dazed. More shots echoed through the clearing.

I looked behind me. Four Wolves bore down on me. The leader lay dead just an arm's length away, killed by the shot that sent me tumbling.

The soldiers manning the gate were shouting and their words burned into my stunned brain. "Code W! Code W!"

I scrambled to my feet and lurched forward, running as fast as I could with my head low. I could hear the Wolves behind me now, gaining speed as they pursued me over the open ground. This early in the morning, they hadn't reached full body temperature yet. I could never outrun a Wolf at full speed, but in the cool mist I pounded ahead, sprinting for safety.

The open gate loomed up in my vision. I was running in a dream, slow motion, dragged down by some heavy force. I saw the faces of the soldiers as they squinted into the sights of their rifles. The muzzle of each rifle jumped as the trigger was pulled, and a tiny puff of smoke issued from the dark tube. The air was full of the sounds of gunfire.

The first soldier backed through the gate and held it wide open. I leaned forward as I ran, feeling the weight of the pack on my shoulders. I smelled the sour tang of the Wolf at my heels.

I stumbled again, pitching forward. I reached out toward the nearest soldier as I fell and he dropped his rifle to grab at my arm. The other soldiers kept firing as I dropped to my knees.

BOOM. One more grenade exploded far away in the tree line.

The soldier pulled me up by the straps of my pack and together we lurched through the gate.

The others dropped back behind us, and I heard the rusty

squeal of the metal closing behind us.

"All clear!" shouted one of them, and the lights of Eden dimmed for a moment as the remaining power surged back through the wires.

The Wolves pulled up short, but the lead beast slid right into the live wires. Sparks showered us and we smelled the burning flesh as the last of Eden's power electrocuted the 'saur, the surge sputtering out all the lights in the camp. The Wolf behind it bounced unharmed off the wires.

I shrugged the pack off my shoulders and gave a weak nod as a soldier opened it. His eyes widened and his mouth fell open when he saw the power core inside. His gaze met mine for a moment before he turned and dashed away toward the generator.

The remaining two Wolves stalked away from the gate, circling Eden's fence in opposite directions.

Soldiers surrounded me, clapping me on the back. I heard their excited voices, but their words meant nothing to me. My vision blurred and I stumbled away from the crowd, weaving blindly through the downed transports and wooden shanties of Eden.

General Enrico followed me. "How many Wolves followed you?" he asked.

My brain took a moment to focus on his words.

"There were four. One shot, one electrocuted." I realized what he meant. "Two left. And they know there's no power."

Gunshots echoed far across the compound. General Enrico took off toward the sound, drawing the pistols from his belt. I took a deep breath and lifted my foot to follow.

Screaming. Right behind me. High pitched screams.

Scat it. Those are kids.

I spun around to see the stumpy tail of a Wolf disappear around the edge of one of our large transports. It was the one we used as a hospital.

By the time I reached the corner, the Wolf was gaining speed. The shrieks of terrified children echoed inside the metal transport shuttle and Mom and another woman were hauling on the huge wooden hatchway. The door was stuck open, rusted in the humid air.

Her eyes met mine and despite her fear, she smiled, then ducked inside.

The Wolf loped toward the open hatchway. I raised my gun and shot it four times fast. The first three bullets bounced off its back plates, but the fourth was lucky and caught it in the soft spot behind its knee. It stumbled and skidded to the ground right in front of the open transport hatch.

I crouched against the hull of the transport twenty feet from the 'saur. I had plenty of rounds but no time to reload. My brain spun as I tried to remember how many shots I had fired since I saw Josh heading straight for the Crab outside the fence. Six? Eight? The guns in each hand held ten shots. I dropped the one that had to be nearly empty and switched the full one to my right hand.

The Wolf rounded on me. Bullets screamed from my gun, mostly bouncing off its hide. I fired and fired, squeezing the trigger. The thunder of the shots ended with a single empty click.

My last bullet hit the Wolf right in the mouth. As I scrambled toward the gun I'd dropped on the ground, the one with maybe two more rounds in it, the Wolf reared back on its hind legs, pawing at the bullet lodged in its jaw.

A deafening roar split the air and the Wolf jumped sideways, the soft underside of its neck exploding in a shower of bloody meat. It crashed to the ground, twitched, then stilled.

Mom emerged from the open transport door, rifle smoking in her hand.

"Holy steaming dino scat! Nice shot, Mom!"

She grinned. "Lived with the General these last few months. He taught me a few things."

Exhaustion flattened me, and I collapsed. Mom rushed over and wrapped her arms around me just as the lights all around the compound sputtered to life.

"The power core," I murmured.

"They got it working," she said.

Children from inside the transport poured out, circling the dead Wolf in wonder. Malia was among them.

"You did it, Cay," Mom said calling me by the babyish nickname I always hated. It didn't sound so bad today. "You and Josh." She raised her head and looked around. "Where is Josh?"

Three soldiers ran up to us and shooed the kids away from the dead Wolf.

"Josh . . ." I stuttered. "You have to find Josh."

They stared at me, then rushed off. A few minutes later, the lights snapped off as the huge gate was opened, and our one remaining tank rumbled out into the jungle to search for my brother.

✦ ✦ ✦

We had gotten the power on just in time.

While Mom and I took down one Wolf, the other had snuck through the wires on the other side of the compound. We lost five more people before a lucky shot brought it down. And it wasn't the only 'saur to notice the power out.

I sat in the hospital while General Enrico ordered our few remaining soldiers to drag the dead Wolves away to be butchered.

"We've never eaten Wolf before," he joked. "These two will keep us fed for a couple of days at least. Shame we didn't get one of the Rexes."

He had been at the fence-line when the Rexes in the jungle heard all the shots. He had seen them come lumbering out of the trees, felt the ground shake under their heavy footsteps. Facing the Wolf, I hadn't even noticed.

"They saw the Wolf come through. Wouldn't have thought they were smart enough to figure it out, but they knew it meant the fences weren't live. Another minute or so . . ." He trailed off.

"It didn't surge." When a 'saur hit the fence, it always surged. Sometimes it killed whatever power source we were using.

"No. One of the transformers blew when the power kicked back on, sparked everywhere. The Rexes saw it, thank the shining stars. Decided we weren't worth the jolt today. Headed back for the jungle. Eden lives another day."

I sighed. "And then what?"

Mom dabbed antiseptic onto the scabs that covered my body. The sting kept my mind off the waiting, listening for the return of the tank. "Then we just . . . keep going," she said. Her eyes kept wandering to the transport's door, hoping Josh would walk through it.

"We have one power core," I said, wincing as she dabbed a wound under my armpit. "How long can we last? One more 'saur rushes the fence and the power surges out. No more Eden base."

General Enrico shook his head. "Caleb's right. We have to find a better situation. Somewhere safe."

Images floated through my exhausted brain. Somewhere safe. Somewhere high in a mountain where 'saurs couldn't climb.

"I know where we can go."

The lights died, signaling the power cut that allowed the gate to be opened. Mom dropped the antiseptic-soaked rag and we dashed outside, blinking in the morning sunlight.

Our huge tank rumbled through the gate.

Mom grabbed my hand as the top hatch popped open.

Josh stuck his head out the hole, face split in a grin. "Hey, Mom. Hey, Squirt. What do you say we move this show to the mountains?"

CHAPTER 36

It took two days to make the trip. Josh and I had left my sat trans with Sara in the caves, and its charge died halfway through the conversation with her that we were coming. All of us.

We took the children first. With one power core to charge two shuttles and keep the fence live, we were cutting it very close.

"People first, then equipment," General Enrico shouted. Everyone scurried around, collecting what we thought was most important in case the power didn't allow everything to go. Once Malia was safely shuttled away, I helped Mom pack up the medical supplies.

"They're not as important as the food," she said. "But we'll take all we can."

The caves would keep us safe, but as far as I had explored, they were nothing but hollowed-out rock. Nothing to eat, and nowhere for our few remaining sheep to forage. We'd still have to brave the jungle on hunting trips. General Enrico was sending all the extra wire ahead, in hopes of staking out a bit of land at the mountain's base where we could grow our crops. But at least we could sleep in safety.

Mom and her medical supplies were on the last shuttle run.

"This is all the power we have," said the pilot. "We'll make it back to the caves, but not back here again."

I had volunteered to be part of the final squad. We watched the shuttle sail away over the trees, taking the last of our power with it. Four of us stood in the quiet compound, suddenly noticing the sounds of the forest without the buzz of the electric wire.

"'Saurs'll be here soon," said General Enrico looking out across the remains of our camp. "They've been watching."

We piled into the tank and rumbled out through the open gate. I peered through the little porthole, reminded of the day I'd first left these fences. Had it only been a week? I felt at least a decade older. The tank bumped through the forest, its vibration obscuring the footfalls of the Rex that had been sniffing around the south fence-line.

It's all yours, I thought. The empty transports. The lean-to shelters. Eden Base was returning to the jungle. We're cave people now.

No one had heard from Shiro in three days. We all knew he was probably dead by now, and we were cutting it close on power to shuttle everyone to the caves. But I convinced General Enrico that even though it was three hours out of our way by tank, we had to look.

He wasn't where we left him.

Half the tree he'd been sitting on was gone, the remainder jutting out over the river like an accusing finger pointing right at me. Too slow. You were too slow and now he's dead. His sat trans battery was out of charge, but it still had a live beacon, and we followed it downriver nearly a kilometer. When we were within a few meters of the beacon, we popped the top of the tank open. I was the first out.

"Shiro?" I called, scanning the forest around the riverbank. My trans homed in on his and I followed its blinking light into a hollow under the riverbank. Shiro lay there facedown, unmoving, the General's makeshift splint still tight on his leg.

I knelt down by his body and laid a hand on my friend.

"Fly free, Shiro," I whispered.

He was still warm.

Stars. My pulse pounded in my ears. Please please please.

I rolled him over.

His eyelids fluttered.

I popped my head up over the hollow and hissed toward the tank. "General Enrico! He's here!"

Shiro was barely conscious as we dragged him up the bank. It took all four of us to get him into the tank, and I cradled his head in my lap the whole way back to the caves.

By the time we arrived, the caves were a hive of activity. Someone directed me to the room Mom and Malia had picked for themselves. I poked my head in.

"Mom, we need you. Shiro's alive!"

She darted past me out the passage toward the room where all her medical equipment was piled up. I knew he was in good hands.

I knelt on the cave floor next to Malia.

"We made it," I said.

Malia plopped into my lap.

"Hey, Mali. You forgot this," I said. I pulled an old worn blanket out of my pack. She had brought it down from Horizon and slept with it every night, its edges frayed and soft. Somehow it had been left behind in the frenzy of packing. She grabbed it and laughed. The sound lifted my heart.

I figured I would bunk in here, but Malia pointed to an adjoining room.

"Mom says you're too old to stay in here with us," she said. "Your room's in there. Mom says you can keep an eye on us."

★ ★ ★

We spent the following weeks exploring our new home. Squads of us probed deeper into the mountain, mapping out the endless corridors of the cave system. We used up a lot of our precious paper until one night I noticed Sara squatting in the room where the birdman's mummy still lay undisturbed.

"What are you doing here?" I asked her. I hadn't seen much of her since we all arrived, and had been too busy to wonder where she was.

"Translating," she said. She gestured around the room. "He left us a key. He drew it all out in pictograms . . . what the scratch marks mean. His language."

I studied the walls of the little room where images of bird men accompanied more of the strange, scratchy writing. My eyes were drawn to a familiar shape painted on most of one wall. I held up the paper in my hand, comparing the images.

"It's a map." I said. "A map of the caves."

Sara looked at the paper I held. "That's exactly what it is."

"Can you read this yet? There's writing all over it."

She shook her head. "I'm working on it. I'll let you know."

★ ★ ★

Two months after we arrived in the caves, we gathered in the great hall. The blue twinkle of the glowworms coating the cave's stalactite ceiling made us feel like we were sitting outside beneath the stars.

We had added to the bird people's paintings.

On the farthest wall of the cave, we added names.

Every name we could remember of the people who were on board Horizon when we entered orbit. All those unaccounted for, who didn't land in Eden with us and must surely be dead by now.

All those lost in the early days when this harsh planet and its inhabitants tried to kill us all. Soldiers, engineers, scientists. The members of Josh's ill-fated mission.

Viktor and Raj, Cara's dad, Mr. Hague, all lost when our shuttle crashed.

Jack. Brent. General Carthage.

Their names were painted on these safe walls. Their lives

wouldn't be forgotten.

I ran my fingers over the cool stone wall as I entered the hall and sat on the floor near the front of the crowd. Some people had brought chairs or cushions, but most of us sat on blankets on the smooth stone. I looked around at all the familiar faces.

Mom sat near the far wall on a bench with Malia cuddled at her side. Mom smiled when she caught my eye, and gave me an encouraging nod. I wiped my sweaty hands on my pants leg and looked back toward the front of the cave.

Shiro nudged me from behind. "Big night tonight, buddy."

I grinned at him. He still looked awful, and Mom said he might always limp, but thanks to the General's splint, he wouldn't lose his leg. He hadn't yet told anyone about his days alone on the river, and I didn't push him. But since the day we found him on the riverbank, he'd always called me "buddy." No more "Squirt."

General Enrico spoke from the front of the room. "Welcome, friends. Take your seats and let's get started."

The murmuring quieted as his voice echoed through the space.

"We gather today to honor and remember those lost when our home planet was destroyed. Without the cooperation of all Earth's scientists, all governments and all peoples, mankind would have been lost forever. We, the descendants of the brave heroes who embarked on a two hundred year voyage to an unknown future, give thanks that through the sacrifice of the world, humans will persevere."

My eyes glazed over. These words were the same every year, spoken on Earth Day, the day we predicted the Earth must have crashed into Jupiter and been destroyed. I didn't really need to hear the ceremonial thanksgiving lecture to be grateful for my life here.

"And now let's hear it for Caleb Wilde, who found our safe haven in the mountains." The sound of a hundred people clapping startled me back to the present. General Enrico motioned for me to step up to the front of the cave and address the crowd. I sweated in the dim cool of the cavern.

I was supposed to make a speech. My throat tasted sour as I shuffled forward to stand next to General Enrico.

"Thank you, General," I began. He nodded, encouraging. I scanned the faces of the crowd. Everyone was beaming at me. I swallowed and spoke again.

"We've been through a tough three years here. We've all lost people we loved." I looked down at my shoes for a moment. "But this place . . . this is where we belong. It's still a struggle, but if our ancestors could see this place, I think they'd be happy for us."

I cleared my throat.

"But we wouldn't be here without the guidance of one man. He kept us alive at Eden base, he found the power we needed, he taught me how to survive in the forest. And he died without knowing his sacrifice would help save us all. So I hereby declare this place be forever known as Carthage, in honor of the General who made it possible."

"Carthage!" roared the crowd. General Enrico clapped me on the shoulder, and I returned to my seat. I looked over to Mom and saw her wiping tears from her cheeks.

CHAPTER 37

The crowd quieted down, and General Enrico spoke again.

"We are fortunate to be here, and fortunate to have a special treat tonight. Sara Arnson, will you please come forward?"

Sara stood up and joined the General.

"As you all know, I've been studying the writings and pictures on the walls of these caves since the day Caleb found them." She glanced at me, and I grinned at her. She'd done little else from the moment she first saw the ancient paintings left by the strange birdman mummy. "It's taken me all these months, and I had to guess a bit, but tonight I'd like to tell the story of the bird people that's written on these walls around us."

The crowd murmured. We had left the birdman where he

died clutching his bowl of paint. Someone fenced off the room to keep the smaller children out, but everyone had peeked inside to see the dry old corpse with its odd beak and taloned feet. Stories had been made up about his origin, and everyone had a theory. But tonight it seemed we would finally hear the truth.

Sara read from a sheaf of papers she had scribbled, months of painstaking work to decipher a language no human had ever seen or heard. The drawings in the mummy room unlocked the code, and she had transcribed her way around the huge cave. She admitted filling in a lot of the details herself, but she was certain she understood the gist of the history painted all around us. The huge cave was silent as we all leaned in to hear Sara's words.

"We came here for sanctuary. Our home planet became too crowded, too barren as we used up our natural resources. War and famine threatened our existence as food grew scarce. We had to find new worlds, new lands to spread our species across the galaxy. Ships went out from the homeworld and we came here." The crowd nodded. We understood.

"We were awestruck by the abundance of life. Never had our kind seen so much water, such lush forests. We landed near a great sea and opened our hatchways to breathe in the moist air. But this world is full of monsters, beasts of evolution gone from our planet for millions of years."

I had been shocked when Sara first told me this bit. She and I had talked a lot more these last few weeks, bonded by our journey through the forest.

Sara continued.

"We fled into our ships and circled the planet, searching for a refuge from the monsters. We found these fertile valleys, and we made our homes in these safe caves. We felt at home within the rocks, and we dug out our small city. We planted our native fruit trees and prepared the roosting grounds. When the time was right, we laid our eggs in the warm soil. But the eggs didn't hatch. We moved the roosts away from the damp ground into the dry caves, and again we laid our eggs. But still, they lay dormant. No chicks emerged, and when we opened the eggs we found our young undeveloped, stunted, dead.

"We prowled through the forest outside in the dead of night, collecting the eggs of the monsters. Their shells were soft and moist, while ours were hard and smooth. Their eggs hatched on the damp soil, and we killed the young before they could kill us. Again we tried, and again, but there is something in the humid air of this world, or the water we drink, or the soil that grows our food. Something here will not allow us to breed. Our species cannot continue here. And so we must leave this place to the monsters."

Sara paused and turned over the page she was reading. No one said a word.

"I watched the ships sail away into the sky, carrying my people to some other world. I hope they find a haven to live and breed and flourish. But some of us are too old to travel with them. We would not live to see a new world and do not wish to die in the cold void of space. So we will remain here for what days we have left."

Sara lifted her eyes from the paper. "He went on for a time about his homeworld, about his family. But here are his final words." She turned back to the page.

"And now I am the last. My aged companions have flown free from their bodies and I have buried them one by one. Only I remain here in this beautiful planet of death. Soon I will join them in the night sky. I do not fear death, for it is my reward. I have written our story here for any who might come after us. I hope this place is more welcome to your kind than it was to mine."

We sat in silence for a moment, caught up in the spell of the birdman's last words. I knuckled away the moisture that threatened my eyes, sorrow for all those lost here, bird people and human.

General Enrico broke the silence and bade us good night. We stood up, stretching in the somber room. I imagined the birdman all alone, the last of his people, painting his message on the wall in hope that someday some intelligent life might read his words and know his story.

"You sure found us an amazing place."

My brother threw his arm around my shoulder.

"I wonder what would have happened if the bird people's eggs had hatched," I said. "They would have been living here all this time. They would have been here to meet us. Things might have been so different."

Josh smiled. "Maybe. Maybe they were worse than the 'saurs. Might have killed us all."

"No," I shook my head. "I've seen his face. The birdman was all right." I laughed.

Erik limped up to us. "That was some story."

"I wonder how much of that Sara really read? She has to have made some of it up," Josh said.

"Not much," I answered. "She showed me some of the letters, how she pieced it together from the drawings. Pretty amazing stuff."

Josh yawned. "Sure something to think about. Goodnight, little bro."

"'Night," I answered and watched him help Erik through the crowd. They shared a room in the cave system. Erik told me Josh still had nightmares about the Rexes outside the fence. He dreamed he wasn't fast enough, couldn't get the last grenade thrown in time, couldn't make it up the tree to safety. I had those nightmares, too.

I walked over to where Mom still sat with Malia, murmuring greetings to everyone I passed.

"Ready to turn in?" I asked them.

Mom smiled. I helped her up off the bench. She was getting bigger every day. I patted her swelling belly.

"Good thing we're not bird people. You don't have to lay an egg that won't hatch." Malia giggled and mom smiled.

"It's a good name, son," she said. When we finished shuttling all our people, our livestock, our medical equipment to the safety of the caves, General Enrico had suggested we call this place "Paradise." But I thought "Carthage" was a better name for this new city, and he agreed. Tonight it became official. The new little brother or sister my mom was carrying would never know his famous father, but when the child was old enough, I would tell the story.

I walked between my mom and my little sister, an arm around each one. We passed the painted walls, the story of a people who couldn't live on this planet. I touched the flaking paint as we strolled past it. We weren't like the birdmen. Maybe we were the only humans left in the universe, but here in Carthage we would find a way.

AFTER EDEN

Sara shook me awake. Her words were still ringing in my ears, the story of the birdmen. I'd been dreaming about them, scuttling through these caves, pursued by a pack of Wolves. My heart was still pounding as I blinked into her flashlight.

"What? What?" I muttered.

"The map," she said. "Caleb, you have to show me where this is on the map." She thrust a pile of papers into my face and I batted them away.

"In the morning, okay?"

"No, now," she insisted. She hauled the blanket off me and I shivered in the chill.

I pulled on a shirt and followed her out of my cavern room, grabbing my own belt and flashlight. "What's so important?"

"Just show me this," she said. She held the papers under her light and pointed to a section of the map.

I took it from her and held it up, turning it in my hands. "Here?"

"There," she confirmed.

"We can't get there," I said, turning to head back toward my bed. "It's down a couple of levels and the tunnel just ends. Rock fall." I knew the tunnel she meant. Sometimes a breath of air wafted up those stairs, but the cave led nowhere.

She held up the paper again. "Caleb, I've been working on this language for weeks. And studying the map the birdman painted. We have to get through there."

"Why?"

"Just . . . just get some guys and meet me at the top of the stairs." She trotted off down the corridor. "Oh, and tools. Bring tools. Whatever heavy stuff you can find." She disappeared and left me shaking my head.

Who am I going to wake up? This is nuts.

I found two soldiers making nightly rounds and woke Josh and Erik. We grabbed some of the farming equipment that was currently unused, since the shuttle flights had used all the power core's charge, dashing our hopes of wiring off some land to plant our crops. Every day we sent troops out to hunt and gather, and to bring back armloads of forage for the sheep. The 'saurs were learning where we came down now, and we had lost three more people since the move.

Sara was standing at the top of the staircase. "Feel that?" She turned her cheek to the moving air in the corridor. "We have to clear the tunnel."

We grumbled, but Sara had been our teacher when we were little kids. It was habit to follow her orders, so we trudged down the stairs to the pile of rocks that blocked the tunnel's end.

"Here!" she cried, staring at the map in her hand. "Move

these rocks!"

It took two hours. As we pulled down the rocks and rubble that blocked the way, her excitement seeped into us all. Fresh air blew into the tunnel, more and more with each rock we hauled out.

Finally it was clear enough at the top to wiggle through. I pulled myself up and over the remaining pile of rocks, tumbling down the other side. The rest of the guys followed, except for Erik. Josh helped Sara down the pile, and we shone our lights down the newly revealed tunnel.

"This way!" She held the map in front of her and dashed down the passage.

We turned a corner and stopped, snapping off our flashlights. Light streamed into the cavern.

The tunnel opened with a wide mouth onto a small rocky plateau. Stretched out in front of us, bordered by the mountains on all sides, a green valley was still in the shadow of early dawn. The sky was fully light, but the sun had not yet risen over the high, steep crags all around us.

My heart skipped. Open air meant 'saurs, and none of us had brought a gun. We stood and listened, peering out over the valley. Wide grassy fields were dotted with copses of trees, and a large lake glittered in the middle.

We waited and watched, barely breathing.

Nothing drank at the water's edge. Nothing stomped through the open fields.

"Is it possible?" I murmured.

Sara looked around the high mountains surrounding us.

"They can't get in. They can't climb those mountains. Look, there's snow at the top."

We looked, and she was right. The peaks were so high that even in the heat of Tau Ceti e, white snow capped them. 'Saurs couldn't possibly get over the tops. If they weren't here now, and the longer we stared the more we became convinced they weren't, then they weren't coming.

Sara had tears in her eyes when she turned to look at us. "This is it. This is Eden."

"Carthage," I corrected her, and we burst into laughter.

The morning sun peeked over the mountaintops and we stood for a moment, soaking in the light. Together we climbed down from the cave mouth and into the green valley, our new home.

NEVER MISS A FUTURE HOUSE RELEASE!

Sign up for the Future House Publishing email list:
www.futurehousepublishing.com/beta-readers-club

Connect with Future House Publishing

www.facebook.com/FutureHousePublishing

www.twitter.com/FutureHousePub

www.youtube.com/FutureHousePublishing

www.instagram.com/FutureHousePublishing

Acknowledgements

I offer heartfelt thanks to all those who helped bring Horizon Alpha to life:

To Ted, who started my love of dinosaurs with the 1970s plastic dino playset. We didn't know dimetrodon and tyrannosaurus couldn't possibly have been friends. We didn't care.

To Mom and Dad for encouraging my love of science.

To my trusted readers Naomi Hughes, Donnie McGovern, Andrew Millard, and Jessica Shroyer, who first followed me to Tau Ceti e.

To L.L.McKinney and the Pitch Slam family for encouragement when I needed it.

To my amazing agent Carly Waters for believing in me.

To my friends at Cincinnati Fiction Writers. You're my kind of crazy.

To Heather, Ami, and Ryan for incredible support at Future House Publishing, to Jeff for coordinating the gorgeous book cover, and to Emma and Mandi for polishing up the Horizon for its long voyage.

And to my patient husband Andrew for undying support of this new phase of my life. You married a vet. I'm so glad you've stayed with the writer.

About the Author

When not dreaming of distant worlds, D.W. Vogel is a veterinarian at Animal Care Centers in Cincinnati, where she has practiced companion animal medicine and surgery since 1997. She started writing in 2011 while undergoing chemotherapy for breast cancer, suddenly realizing that the time to write that novel was no longer "someday." Chemo, radiation, and ten surgeries later, she's back to running marathons, SCUBA diving, endurance cycling, and wishing she cared about gardening so her yard could be as nice as her neighbors'. Wendy's first fantasy novel, Flamewalker, debuted in 2015 from Word Branch Publishing.

Her husband, Andrew, is a business analyst by day, professional chef by night. Together they are parents to a houseful of special needs pets.

If you liked this book, I'd love to hear.
Reviews keep me writing.
Find *Horizon Alpha: Predators of Eden* online and leave me a review.

Made in the USA
Lexington, KY
13 March 2018